STOLEN
a MASON GRAY *case*

by

WILLIAM C. MARKHAM

"The world is full of obvious things which nobody
by any chance ever observes."

– Sherlock Holmes

Prologue

Shamash ran. Rain pounded the packed earth around him, making the ground slick beneath his sandaled feet. Lightning sliced through the night sky, illuminating stark pillars of rock hidden in the darkness. Thunder split the air. Such storms were rare in this sun-baked land, but the timing of this one was fortuitous. Beneath his robes, he clutched the idol tightly lest it tumble from his grasp as he fled through the night.

He was likely the last priest left alive, the others slaughtered by the Usurpers. The sound of clashing weapons rose above the storm, and he knew the soldiers fought desperately so he could escape. They would be slaughtered as well. It was only a matter of time. They were outnumbered three to one.

The temple had fallen not long ago. It was their last stronghold. The Usurpers had hunted them all down, vowing to destroy every last remnant of the "false god" Shamash worshiped. The priests had been reluctant to flee, believing their faith would save them, but Shamash knew they were lost.

His last hope was to find someplace safe to hide the idol. Centuries ago it had been given to the first priest, a gift from Hadad himself. Its power was subtle but great. If it were taken, it could be used against the one who created it. As long as it was safe, though his own life might be for-

feit, his god would live on.

Shamash stumbled over the loose scree littering the hillside. The driving rain might impede his pursuers, but it hindered his own attempt at escape as well. He regained his footing and scrambled on, climbing higher. The hills surrounding the temple were rife with caves. If he could find one before he was spotted, he might be able to escape.

Shouts carried by the wind found his ears. They did not speak his language. He had to hurry. He had been spotted as he fled from the temple, but the soldiers cut off pursuit. If they had fallen already, the enemy would be upon him soon.

He grew frantic in his desperation. His head swiveled from side to side, searching for some dark hole to climb into.

Lightning flashed again, and he saw it: a black smudge against the gray stone. It was halfway down the rise to his right. He altered course and picked up speed, half running, half falling as he went. At some point in his mad dash, his feet couldn't keep up, and he pitched forward, landing on the jagged stones and skidding headfirst down the slope.

He felt the skin on his arm tear, and as he picked himself up, the rainwater sheeting off of him was tinged pink with blood.

Still, he ran on.

The shouts of the Usurpers grew louder behind him.

At last, he reached the dark blemish on the land-scape—the opening in the hillside. It was large enough to let a man crawl through, but not much bigger. He wriggled through; his robe caught and ripped on the stone, but he paid it no heed. Still, he clutched the idol with one hand, the other covered in blood, leaving smears on the ledges behind.

Inside, he found shelter from the rain and wind, but he did not stop. He pushed deeper into the cave, knowing he left a trail a blind man could follow, but he was out of options. Perhaps if he went far enough, they would eventually give up pursuit.

His luck did not hold. The cave extended just over a hundred feet before the ceiling sloped down too far to allow further movement.

This was it. He slumped down, putting his back to the cave wall.

Blood dripped from his arm. Wind howled. Rain fell. Shamash prayed.

He prayed not for his life, but for his god to protect the idol. He would be heard; he knew that. Being this close to the idol, its power granted him that much, at least.

There was a brilliant flash from the mouth of the cave as lightning lanced down from the heavens, striking the hill outside. Thunder boomed as the vacuum left by superheated air was suddenly filled. The resulting explosion shook the ground. Stone cracked above Shamash's head as a great slab broke loose.

It shifted, then fell, breaking into several pieces before crashing down. Giant chunks of rock landed between Shamash and the opening to the outside, sealing off the entrance. They also sealed him inside, leaving no way out.

As the dust from the collapse settled, Shamash looked around at his tomb. No one would ever find him here. Not him and not his precious idol. His prayers had been answered.

1

Two months ago I learned that vampires were real.

Tonight, I was hunting a mushroom thief. Life can be weird like that.

I slipped between two stainless-steel racks of trays filled with crab rangoon and ducked around a corner. The kitchen was a cacophony of clanking pots, pans, and utensils too numerous to name, as the staff prepared the third course for the hungry diners on the floor above. I snuck down a short hallway to the closet where my stuff was stashed, ditched the culinary attire I was wearing, and hastily donned my street clothes—complete with trench coat and fedora. I was done playing dress-up and wanted to be comfortable for what I was about to do.

The owner had hired me to investigate the night manager who was showing signs of wealth that he shouldn't be able to afford on his salary; things like a fancy new car and thousand-dollar tailored suits. He brought me in because he didn't want the establishment's name besmirched if the goings-on were less than reputable.

I ran all the usual checks. While I can't access bank account records or credit card transactions like the authorities can, there are other ways of discovering financial irregularities. Large purchases such as vehicles and property must be registered with the DMV, city, county, or state of ownership. Those, I can get. Of course, simple surveillance is the best way to get a sense of how much someone spends. Do they eat at expensive restaurants frequently? How often do they buy new and pricey clothes or accessories? What kinds of deliveries are made to their homes? My observations indicated that the manager was most certainly living above his means. But I hadn't found a reasonable source of the income boost. No great-aunt had kicked-off and left a sizable estate behind. He hadn't recently married into money. There wasn't anything above board. That left something shady.

This was my favorite part of the job. I love hitting the streets—or the high-rises— looking for pieces of the puzzle that will solve a case.

Years ago, when I worked for the Chicago Police Department, I did much the same thing. Except back then, there were rules I had to follow. You know, all those civil rights cops aren't supposed to violate. It didn't matter what kind of incriminating evidence I found if I hadn't found it the right way.

Now, in the private sector, I didn't have to worry so much about that. My clients paid me to find information, or people, or whatever. As long as I didn't break any laws myself, I could get it however I wanted.

I had followed the manager for several days, and it appeared he was taking meetings with other chefs around the city, but I didn't know why.

So I had to get closer. My cover was simple: a new kitchen employee to be trained for a week. This allowed me to get inside the restaurant and poke around without anyone becoming too suspicious.

I'm an observant person. I pay attention to details. I see things that others miss. Which is why it only took me two nights to pick up on the scam.

The restaurant, Moxy, is an upscale place on the twentieth floor of one of the downtown hotels with views overlooking Grant Park and the lake. They specialize in high-end, gourmet cuisine. One of their most notable ingredients are truffles. They're in a lot of dishes and come with a weighty price tag. One of the cooks was skimming from the truffle stash.

Pinching an entire truffle from the stock would have been a dead give-away to the owner since they were so valuable. So the cook had to be sneaky about it. The prized fungus had to be thinly sliced or grated when added to a dish, so for each one he prepared, he'd let a gram or so fall to the counter. These cast-offs were collected and handed off to the night manager.

A few grams of truffle a night wouldn't be missed and wouldn't throw up any red flags during inventory. Of course, they'd be difficult to sell like that too, so I didn't have all the pieces yet.

Just minutes ago, there'd been a handoff. Now I had to track down the manager and see what he was doing with the pilfered product.

I poked my head out of the closet door and glanced down the hall. I suspected the manager was in the walk-in cooler. Between here and there servers waited near an elevator to deliver the third course. Now that I had changed, I needed to stay out of sight. I waited until the doors thunked open, and the servers wheeled the cart of savory delights on. When the doors closed again, I made my move. Double-timing it down the hall to the corner, I put my back against the wall, and peered around to see the walk-in cooler. The door was ajar.

I cast around, looking for a better hiding spot. Barging in on whoever was in there wasn't a good idea. I needed to wait until they left, then snoop. Of course, if I was discovered lurking in the hallway, that would be just as bad.

The interesting thing about the service areas of these buildings is that there's always stuff being stored anywhere there's available floor space. Most of it's on wheels or strapped to a dolly so it can be moved easily. These areas are off limits to guests, and aesthetics aren't a consideration when designing them. It's all about practicality. A broken industrial washer just beyond the entrance to the cooler would provide the perfect cover.

I slid down the hallway and took up position behind the stainless-steel monster. I fished the phone out of my pocket and opened the camera; It wasn't the greatest way of taking pictures. I tend to go on the cheap side when buying a phone and camera quality is one of the first sacrifices to be made. Fortunately, at close range, it didn't matter.

Within minutes, the night manager came out of the walk-in and secured the door behind him. I snapped a few photos from my hidey-hole, and he didn't even look around suspiciously. He was the manager; he had every right to be in the walk-in.

He strode back toward the kitchen, and when he was out of sight, I let myself into the cooler.

At first, being in a walk-in cooler is refreshing. It's not a freezer. It functions more like a giant refrigerator for fresh fruits and vegetables. The temperature was right around 38 degrees, so I had a few minutes before I started to feel the full-force of the cold.

Shelves lined the walls. I could see greens of all kinds stored in plastic tubs, a few root vegetables, and trays of what looked like lamb quarters. That wasn't what I was looking for.

Then I saw a shelf of dressings and other condiments, so I directed my attention there. I rearranged the big plastic jars of mayo and pickles and spotted something in the back—glass jars full of oil with dark shapes floating around. I pulled one to the front for closer inspection. I'm not a culinary guru, but it looked like the truffle scraps were being used to infuse olive oil. I did know that oil like this went for about six bucks an ounce, and these were gallon jars. Even if he was selling it at a discounted rate, which he probably was, the manager could easily make a grand on these three alone. Especially since he wasn't paying for the truffles to begin with. I wasn't sure how long the infusion process took, but if he'd been doing this for a while, it could account for his additional income.

I snapped a couple of photos, then put the jars back in place. The cooler shielded the signal from my phone, so I'd have to send them later.

That's when the searing pain stabbed into the back of my eyeballs.

My vision swam and I dropped to a knee, clutching the sides of my head.

The headaches started just after I'd learned about the vampires. Have I mentioned that yet? I had a run-in with a couple of them while I was working a case. A girl was missing and I tracked her to an old warehouse where she was kept sedated while her blood was harvested. At least, that's what it looked like to me. The people who took her got really pissed off and tried to lure me into a trap by kidnapping my mentor and business partner, Frank.

There were two of them. Both were incredibly strong and super fast. They shrugged off injuries that would send a normal person to the hospital for a week;

blows that should have been lethal weren't. I found that out the hard way. However, they had a weakness to silver. I used that to my advantage and put both of them down. But not before they killed Frank and nearly mashed my skull to pulp.

Those injuries healed with surprising speed. No one could explain it, but I was pretty sure it had to do with the strange dreams I'd been having. In them, I saw pulsing cords of red and blue energy flowing around me. Touching them had strange effects. The blue ones gave me a sense of peace and joy and seemed to help me heal. The red ones made me angry; filled me with rage and incredible strength. I didn't know how any of it was possible, but after tangling with vampires, my sense of what was possible had been shattered.

The headaches started soon after. I didn't know if they were a result of the beating I'd taken or if they also had something to do with the dreams. Whatever the reason, they were becoming a major problem, and this was the worst one yet.

I knelt on the floor of the cooler for a few minutes —the cold helping to dull the pain. When the throbbing eased, I used the shelving to regain my feet. The pain wasn't gone yet, but it was bearable.

I had what I came for. It was time to leave.

Stumbling to the door, I half fell into it, using the safety handle to push it open. I stepped into the corridor

—and came nose to nose with the night manager. He was a pretty big guy. I had maybe an inch on him. I think he worked out, too. Behind him stood the cook that had handed off the truffles. He was shorter. And fatter. He also held a cleaver in a meaty fist.

Surprise registered on the manager's face.

"What the hell were you doing in there?"

"Headache," I said. "The cold helps."

He looked me up and down. "Why are you dressed like that? You're still on the clock."

I didn't have a clever response. His expression darkened and I could tell jig was up.

I could hit him. He'd probably go down with one punch. I wasn't sure about Cookie though. He looked like he could hold his own. Of course, they'd done nothing but scowl at me. Violence wasn't called for yet. I doubted, however, they were going to let me just walk away. So, I did the only thing I could: I turned and ran.

I covered about twenty feet before the shock dissipated and the two came running after me. There was an emergency exit door at the end of the corridor. I slammed it open without breaking stride, coming into the stairwell. Up or down? I considered the question as I ran. Though I had a several second lead, I'd lose it trying to run down nineteen floors. I was sure the manager would catch me, and I didn't like the idea of being caught in tight quarters with no witnesses. So instead, I went up, taking the stairs three at a time.

The door slammed open behind me, and they paused briefly before hearing my footfalls above. The manager shouted at me to stop.

When I reached the landing, I yanked the door open and dashed down the much narrower hall back toward the service elevator. An ice machine and drink station were set up beside a set of swinging double doors that I guessed would open into the dining room. That's where I was headed. I doubted the manager would make a scene in front of all the guests, and I'd be able to figure out my next move there.

The elevator doors ground open and a server wheeled a cart out into the hallway at the same time the manager burst through the door behind me. I picked up the pace, not wanting to get cut off. It was close. I slid through the doors just as the servers got there.

As soon as I stepped into the dining room, I slowed to a casual stroll. In contrast to the bright lights of the kitchen and service area, the lighting in here was dim; the walls painted a dark burgundy. Windows lined the far wall, giving diners a nice view of the city. I heard a commotion and raised voices behind as the manager and servers tried to sort out who was going through first. Every head in the dining room turned to see what was going on, but I paid them no mind. I wove my way between tables, heading for the exit.

I grabbed my phone and checked to see if it had service. It did. I pulled up the photos I'd taken and quickly sent them to my client. Now, even if I got caught, the job was done. I had no intention of being caught, however, and the traffic jam at the doors gave me a few extra seconds to get out of sight.

I nodded to the host as I left the dining room and turned the corner on the way to the guest elevators. I pushed the button then started running again. I hadn't done any snooping up here and didn't know the layout, but I figured that being a hotel, another stairwell was around somewhere. There was. It only took a minute to find, and I took the stairs two at time, making my way down twenty floors.

I felt pretty good about the evening's outcome as I wound through the maze of hallways on the first floor looking for an exit. I'd found the dirt my client was after, hadn't broken any laws myself, adrenaline had killed my headache, and I'd avoided any kind of violence. Wanting to keep it that way, I decided against using the main lobby. I hadn't seen or heard anyone on my way down but figured they might be waiting for me to come that way, so I was looking for a back door. Turning the corner, I found one–excellent.

Cold wind and snow swirled about me as I stepped outside into the night. It was mid-December, and the air had long since stopped being brisk and become bitter with a side of frigid. I looked around to get my bearings. Wandering through the hotel had screwed with my sense of direction. A quick glance up and down the street told me I was at the back of the building, not far from the service entrance where my night had begun. Perfect. My car was parked two blocks west of here.

Driving was a relatively new addition to my life. But then, a lot had changed over the last two months. For most of my adult life, I'd been a loner. I had few friends, no family in the city, and, other than the occasional short-lived romance, no love life. But when Frank died, I grew a lot closer to his widow, Nancy, and their two daughters, Alice and Maggie. I could never take his place, and didn't want to, but I could take more responsibility. Anyway, Nancy gave me Frank's old Buick. She had a much newer car and figured I could use the old one. It had come in handy a time or two, and I certainly appreciate not having to stand in the weather on nights like this. Of course, I still took the train plenty. Sometimes trying to find parking isn't worth it.

I flipped up my collar against the wind, shoved my hands into my pockets, and started walking.

I'd taken ten steps when someone stepped out onto the sidewalk in front of me. He was short. And fat. Crap. It was the cook. He glared at me—then raised his cleaver.

I took my hands out of my pockets and threw

them up, taking a step back. "Whoa, buddy. Calm down."

He spat a string of curses at me in a language I didn't understand.

"Okay, I get that you're upset," I said. "I was just doing my job. It's over now and I'm going home."

"No. You're not," he said and took a step toward me.

Normally, I would have drawn my piece to warn him off, but I'd locked it in the glove box of the Buick before starting the shift. I was just about to turn and run again—I figured I could outdistance him quickly—when someone else stepped outside. A woman with close-cropped hair the color of ink and wearing slim black slacks with a crisp white button-up under a navy pea coat glanced between me and Cookie. "What's going on here?" she asked.

He tensed up at the sound of her voice. "None of your business, woman."

She bristled at his tone, stalked toward him, and launched into a tirade in a foreign language, presumably the one he'd used earlier. He lowered the cleaver and turned to face her. He tried to interrupt, but she was having none of it. I had no idea what she was saying, but the scolding cowed him quickly. When she said her piece, she stood there glaring at him until he huffed in frustration and stormed past her back to the entrance.

When he disappeared from sight, she turned to

leave.

"Thank you," I said. "Things were about to get pretty hairy."

She looked over her shoulder and arched a dark eyebrow. "I'll say." But she kept walking.

She was going my way, so I caught up and walked beside her. "I'm Gray, by the way."

She stopped to face me. "Look, I don't really care who you are. I've had a long day, and that was the last thing I needed."

"I'm sorry, I didn't mean to bother you, but you kind of saved my ass back there and I owe you one."

"Yeah, well..."

"What did you say to him? That was a pretty quick turnaround." I was impressed with how she handled him and didn't mind admitting it.

"I reminded him of his duties to his wife and kids and pointed out that if he went to jail it would kill his mother. Now, if you'll excuse me." She continued down the sidewalk.

I followed behind like a puppy. I knew I should just let her go and forget about the whole incident, but for some reason, I couldn't. "What language was that?"

"Greek."

"Oh." *Shut up, Gray. Leave her be.* "Can I buy you a drink?" *Ugh.*

"No, thanks," she said and picked up the pace a little.

"Okay, but at least take my card." I held it out like a peace offering. "I owe you a favor. If you need anything, give me a call."

She slowed down long enough to take it from my outstretched hand and shove it into a pocket. After that, I stopped. A few seconds later I called after her, "Thanks, again!" *Real smooth, Gray, real smooth.*

2

It wasn't quite ten o'clock when I got back to the Buick—still too early to go home, considering how hyped up I was from the chase—so I decided to go back to the office. I had another project to work on, one that seemed to take up all my spare time these days.

On the drive there, my mind kept going back to the woman I'd just met. I wished I'd gotten her name. I wished I had some way to get in touch with her. I wished I hadn't been so awkward. I knew I shouldn't dwell on it. I'd probably never see her again, but I couldn't shake the thought of her.

She was the type of woman I was drawn to: petite; dark, olive skin; big brown eyes; high, full cheeks that sloped down to a chin that could cut glass.

I sighed, knowing I'd be thinking about her for the next week or two, frustrated there was nothing I could do about it.

I went up the back way to the office, as usual, and our resident alley cat, One-Eyed Willy, meowed at me. He was a scruffy, orange tabby cat with ragged ears and a missing eye. I had a soft spot for him because of the tenacity it took to survive on the streets, and even more so because he saved my life two months ago right here on this very landing. Since then, I made sure to leave a bowl of food and water out for him every day. I bent down and gave him a good scratching behind one mangled ear. A deep rumble sounded in his chest.

I unlocked the door and was about to push it open, when Willy thudded into it with his shoulder. He'd been trying to get in for a while, but I didn't think that would bode well for the tidiness—or smell—of the office.

"Not now, buddy," I said as I moved him out of the way with my foot and slipped inside, closing the door behind me. I could hear his answer through the door as a miffed mewl. A twinge of guilt twisted my heart, but I ignored it and flipped on a light.

The back door opened into the kitchenette and I hurried through and down the hall, past Frank's old office to mine. I dumped my coat on the back of the couch, then pulled out a whiteboard stashed along the wall and wheeled it to the center of the room. Taped to its center was an array of photos and a web of lines drawn between and around them. This was what I'd been working on.

After Ellie McCarthy's kidnapping and Frank's murder, I turned my attention to the CPD. Since being drummed out of the department myself, I had a bone to pick, and the fact they had done so little to investigate these cases stank of corruption so bad I couldn't help but sniff around. I was still in the early stages of the investigation and hadn't found much, but just the attempt was therapeutic.

I examined the faces taped to the board. I had

copies of all the police reports relating to the cases and used them to create a flow chart of those involved. I said each name aloud as I studied their picture, knowing them all by heart at this point.

Detective Rowe was up there. So were several beat cops: Nathan Drury, Doug Kinney, and Damon Rivers. Detectives Bryan Sullivan and Alex Conrad, Sergeant Rhonda Hatfield, Lieutenant Donald Wiggins, and Captain Robin Woods rounded out my cast of players. So far, I had basic information about all of them and was mapping out their connections. I was looking at Conrad the hardest. He was the detective in charge of the McCarthy case and had done next to nothing to investigate it. I needed to know why.

I booted up my desktop and dug into Conrad's life. What I really missed about working for the department was the access to personal information like bank accounts and phone records. I could get them with a subpoena just like the cops, but the likelihood of getting a judge to sign off on it for a private investigator was almost nil, especially since I was investigating the cops. Instead, I turned to social media. People who post frequently leave a neon trail with brightly glowing breadcrumbs everywhere they've been.

Conrad wasn't a frequent poster, but that actually made my job easier. I didn't have to comb through hundreds of pictures looking for places that appeared the most. What I did find were a handful of photos of Conrad and friends hanging out at a local establishment called Smitty's. That was promising. I hadn't been able to talk to anyone involved yet. Perhaps I could drop in and poke around, find out when he was likely to show up, and have a conversation with the guy.

Feeling like I'd made a step in the right direction, I shut the computer down, wrote "Smitty's" next to Conrad's photo on the whiteboard, and flopped onto the couch.

Brenda arrived bright and early the next morning. I'd hired her just after Frank's death—partly to fill the emptiness, partly because I needed help running the place, and partly because I felt responsible for her. She had worked for a crooked real estate company involved with the vampires, though she was in the dark about their true nature. She had provided evidence about the company's other illicit dealings, and the authorities shut them down. I was surprised it happened so quickly. It seemed like a lot of effort had been made to keep them from being discovered in the first place. Whatever the reason, Brenda had been left jobless, and it seemed only right to offer her one.

It was one of the best decisions I could have made. Brenda shot past competence and rocketed into indispensable within the first month. While she still didn't know the ins and outs of the detective business, she knew how to run a *business*. From accounting to marketing, she was streamlining things I never knew Frank was responsible for. And she was a people person. Because she was taking care of the administrative side of things, I was free to do what I do best: investigate. I got results for our clients. She kept them happy. And happy clients give referrals. I was busier than ever and I had Brenda to thank for it.

She roused me from the couch and told me to get cleaned up. I had an appointment at ten with a new client. I pulled a clean shirt out of the coat closet and went in the bathroom for a quick sponge bath. While I was doing that, Brenda put on a pot of coffee.

"Be on your best behavior," she told me after I was dressed and pouring a cup. "This is a big one. You're going to the Field Museum to meet with one of the curators. Go to the east entrance and ask for Dr. Halgrave."

"Field Museum? What's the case?" I asked.

"I don't know. They refused to discuss the details over the phone. Said the doctor would fill you in when you got there."

"Did they say why they chose us?"

"Not exactly. They said they heard you had a reputation for solving tough cases."

"Huh," I said. "Okay. Anything else I should know?"

"Yeah, take the case. Right now, you're going for a consultation. If you accept, they're paying five thousand up front."

I nearly choked on my coffee. That was a lot for a retainer.

"Yeah," she continued. "They really want you on this."

Next, I told Brenda what I'd learned last night at Moxy and that as far as I was concerned, the case was closed. She went back to her office, Frank's old one, to process billing while I finished my cup of coffee. After another trip to the bathroom to make sure I was presentable, I grabbed a pen and notepad and headed for the door.

"Keep your parking stub!" Brenda shouted down the hall. "They validate."

"Thanks!" I shouted back on my way out the door to the Buick. Willy glared at me from the porch the whole way.

3

The Field Museum is the natural history museum in Chicago. It's located along the lake just south of the loop on the museum campus, a sprawling public park, where Soldier Field, the Adler Planetarium, and Shedd Aquarium are also situated. Sue, the T-Rex skeleton is probably the most iconic feature, but it's full of many others: anthropological exhibits, geological collections, and zoological displays. My favorite is the Hall of Gems. I always end up in the darkened room staring at the crystalline beauty created deep in the bowels of the earth, then cut and polished by man into valuable treasures I could never afford.

Multiple theories of what they wanted rattled around my brain on the drive over. I suspected it had something to do with investigating the authenticity or origins of some new acquisition. Of course, there were far more qualified people for that. Or perhaps one of those priceless gems had been stolen and they wanted me to recover it on the DL so the insurance company wouldn't be notified. But honestly, I had no idea what I was walking into.

Mind buzzing, I pulled the long silver sedan into the mostly empty parking lot. The tourists aren't as thick in the winter, but there are always some willing to brave the biting wind for a look at the latest exhibition. I found a spot as close to the building as possible and made for the east entrance.

The main entrance to the museum is an imposing sight of neoclassical architecture with a set of marble steps framed by massive ionic columns. Most visitors use this entrance during business hours. The east entrance, however, is a modern addition at ground level primarily used as handicap access and an entrance for special events. Security's tight. It's always manned by at least one guard and there's a walkthrough metal detector.

I pushed through the door and sidled up to the station where a guard sat reclined in a metal chair behind a small plastic table. Aside from me and the guard, this section of the building was empty. He looked up from his cell phone.

"Morning," he said. "What can I do for you?"

"I have an appointment with a Dr. Halgrave at ten o'clock," I informed him.

"Ah," he muttered, then reached for the walkie-talkie on the table in front of him. He said, "Come in, Cleve, come in." The radio squelched as he released the button.

A moment later there was a response. "Go for Cleve."

"Cleve, this is Rog. I got a visitor down here at East End for Dr. Halgrave."

"Roger that."

The guard turned his attention back to me. "Someone will be down shortly to retrieve you. Empty your pockets and step through the detector, please."

Instead, I took out my PI badge and laid it on the table in front of him. Then I flipped it to my weapon permit so he could get a good look at it. "I'm here on business and don't want to catch anyone off guard. Thought you should know I'm carrying before I step through that thing."

He checked my credentials and narrowed his eyes, suddenly wary.

"Right. You just stay put until someone comes to get you then."

I stood there for what seemed like an hour acting nonplussed. I'm sure it wasn't more than six or seven minutes, but time has a way of dragging in situations like that. The guard just sat there, watching me. I thought he might go back to playing on his phone, but apparently knowing I was packing had him paying attention.

Eventually, a woman in a white lab coat came into view striding down the hallway toward us. I had to work really hard to keep my mouth from dropping open. Black heels defined perfect calves on lightly tanned legs that ran up beneath the coat that draped her trim figure. Long brown hair fell around her shoulders in silky waves. Black glasses straddled the bridge of her nose on a face that should have been in the movies. I swallowed, reminding myself not to stare. Then we locked eyes and she smiled. My heart skipped a beat or four and I heard Roger at the security desk suck in a lungful of air, like he'd forgotten to breathe for a minute. Calling her beautiful would have been like calling Jupiter big.

As she neared, she extended her hand. I was proud that I remembered how a handshake worked, yet appalled at how oafish my meaty paw felt in contrast to her delicate grip. On contact, I felt my knees literally go weak. I also felt the beginnings of a headache take root behind my eyes. A few seconds passed before I realized she was speaking.

"...but, please, call me Meredith."

"Meredith," I stammered. "I'm Gray. It's a pleasure to meet you."

She smiled again. "Thank you for coming. I'm sorry to keep you waiting. If you'll follow me, we can discuss the reason I called." She turned and walked back the way she had come. I glanced at the guard questioningly and he nodded, so I hustled to catch up.

Dr. Halgrave led me past the Underground Adventure and Ancient Egypt exhibits and used a keycard to open a security door off a side corridor. Once through, we wound our way through a warren of starkly lit hallways until we reached an office with her name beside the door. Inside was a small desk with a sleek new computer sitting on top. A low shelf was placed along one wall and held several neatly stacked volumes. Pictures of ancient artifacts and tribal artwork hung neatly on the walls. The office seemed a little too sterile. There were no personal items in view, no clutter to speak of, no evidence that she actually did any work here. She waved me in and I took a seat. She went around behind the desk and sat across from me.

"I'm sorry I couldn't provide your assistant with any details over the phone," she said once she settled in. I was only half-listening. It was hard to concentrate around her. She was beautiful, sure, but there was more to it than that. She exuded a magnetism I couldn't explain. "I felt it would be better to discuss them here. Before we begin, however, I need you to sign a non-disclosure agreement." That got my attention. She opened a drawer, withdrew a sheet of paper, and slid it across the desk so I could see it. "Take your time to read it if you wish, but all it says is that you agree not to discuss anything you learn today with anyone—unless you agree to take the case."

"Alright," I said, glancing over the document. It seemed straightforward so I picked up a pen lying on the desk, signed my name, and slid it back to her.

She picked it up, looked at my signature and said, "Thank you...Mason. May I call you Mason?" I shuddered as a chill ran up my spine. Normally, I didn't like anyone to call me Mason, but the way she said it sounded so natural.

I shrugged and said, "Sure."

She put the paper back in the drawer and laced her fingers in front of her. "As you may know, the Field Museum is home to many artifacts and collections that are not on display to the public." I nodded so she continued. "Some of them belong to private collectors—donors—who loan them to us for extended periods of time for various reasons. We pride ourselves on the ability to care for these items and maintain their condition better than the owners could."

"Okay," I said.

"To the point, then," she said after a brief pause. "An artifact belonging to one of these private collectors has disappeared. We need you to help us find it." Her choice of words was odd.

"What do you mean *disappeared*? Was it stolen, misplaced, what?"

"I suppose the best thing would be to show you the footage." I shrugged and she turned her attention to the computer monitor and clicked the mouse a few times. Then she angled the monitor so I could see it easily. A surprisingly clear image showed a wide angle view of a large room lined with rows of shelves. I saw various items perched on them, though the camera was too far away to make out any detail. There were also several people in lab coats standing in the room.

"This is an image from one of our security cameras in the Collections Resource Center," said Dr. Halgrave. Then she placed the tip of her pen on the screen. "This is the artifact in question." I squinted, focusing on the object at which she pointed, and could discern it was some figurine, but little else. "Pay close attention." She tapped a key, and at first, I thought nothing had happened, but then realized the people in the video were shifting positions slightly, consumed with their own tasks. Someone walked into frame and retrieved a different item off the shelf, then one of the scientists on screen turned, clipboard in hand and moved out of view. This continued for about thirty seconds with several other people moving in and around the field of view. A couple passed by the artifact I was supposed to be watching, but never paused long enough to glance at it, let alone pick it up, but that's when I realized the object was no longer there.

"Wait, stop," I said. Halgrave hit another key and the image froze once more. "How long ago did this happen?"

"Three days ago."

"Did you call the police?"

"Of course. But they are thoroughly baffled. No leads. I've been told you're the best with these sorts of things." It was an amazing compliment—one that I would otherwise brush aside, but I couldn't think of anything to say, so I looked back at the monitor.

"Play it again," I said. She did. This time I ignored everything else in the video and kept my eyes glued to the artifact. A figure passed in front of it and then it was gone. "Pause it."

When the picture froze again, I searched the screen for whoever had obscured the view of the object. On the right-hand side, almost off camera, was what appeared to be a security guard. I pointed at him. "Who's that?"

"That would be Randall Cleaver," replied Dr. Halgrave.

I glanced up at her. "Cleve?"

She smiled. "Yes. And the police picked him out for questioning as well, though it took them a bit longer. He was little help, unfortunately, and though they did a thorough search of his property, nothing was found to suggest he took the artifact. Do you think they were wrong?"

"I'm not sure what to think yet," I told her.

I had her play the video again, this time watching for Cleve and focused on him when he entered the frame. He was walking smoothly along, looking around nonchalantly. He appeared comfortable, at ease. If he was the thief, he was certainly practiced enough not to show nerves. He strode by the artifact without sparing it the slightest look. I'd have to get measurements to be sure, but it looked like he wasn't close enough to the shelf to touch it.

"Are there cameras that cover this area from a different angle?" I asked.

"No, I'm sorry. Some areas have overlap in coverage, but not this one. I assure you, though, that every inch of that facility has video surveillance. I can get whatever footage you'd like to see."

I nodded. Now that I wasn't focused on the video, it was getting hard to concentrate again.

"Can I see the room?"

"Of course. Now?"

I nodded again. She stood and told me to follow her. I tried really hard not to stare at her ass as we walked back down the hallway but failed miserably. She led me to an elevator and once we were aboard, she swiped a keycard in front of a sensor and pushed the button labeled "B".

It was a short ride, the elevator only descending one floor, but when the doors slid open, it felt like we were in a completely different building. A long hallway stretched in front of us, the white walls brightly lit by fluorescent light bars hanging from the ceiling. The black bulbous eyes of two security cameras at either end watched our progress. At the end of the hall, we came to a heavy metal security door. Again, Halgrave swiped her key card in front of a sensor attached to the wall and pulled it open.

On the other side was a security checkpoint in a small square room. A guard sat behind a plastic folding table. He stood and gave us the once-over but said nothing. I assumed he was there to check bags, purses, or other items people took in and out of the Resource Center. After Halgrave swiped her card yet again, she punched a code into a keypad beside the door.

We stepped into another hallway; this one was much longer, perhaps a hundred yards, and lined with doors along one side. We passed all of them, and I glanced through the small windows set in each to see various laboratories. Eventually, we came to a set of double doors set in the opposite wall. These opened into one of the largest, most well-organized storage facilities I've ever seen.

The room was the size of a football field with row upon row of metal shelving that held thousands, if not millions of artifacts. I could tell this was the room from the security video. Dr. Halgrave led me about halfway down and indicated the nearest shelving unit.

"This is where the artifact in question was stored," she told me.

The shelf was chest high. Others, closer to the center of the room, were taller. I approached for a closer inspection.

Dozens of small sculptures, each meticulously labeled, were aligned in neat rows. I hadn't an inkling as to their significance, but it was clear that they were very, very old. The arrangement of the items made it apparent that there was a void, an empty spot where something should have been. More importantly, at least from my perspective, the shelves had no back. I could peer between them and see what lay beyond. It was possible that someone had taken the artifact from the other side, though I had no idea how they'd done it without being seen.

I turned my attention to the wall behind me, looking for the camera that had captured the baffling disappearance. From the angle I had seen, I knew it wouldn't be near the ceiling, which was at least twelve feet high. That high and it would only capture the tops of heads, which would be useless. It would be lower, maybe eight to ten feet, so faces would still be visible in the footage. I spotted it and ran a few sightlines in my head.

"Would it be possible to see the video being recorded now?" I asked.

"I suppose we could arrange that. Why?" Dr. Halgrave asked.

"Just want to test an idea." I walked around to the other side of the shelving unit and crouched down so that my head was below the top. I counted to five, then got down on all fours, like I was crawling. I counted to five again, then dropped to my stomach and did a short belly crawl. Then I stood up and walked back to Dr. Halgrave, who looked at me quizzically. Meeting her gaze, I felt incredibly foolish. Though I'd been certain of what I was doing just a moment ago, my actions now seemed absolutely ridiculous.

I shrugged with a sheepish grin and looked around the massive room again, as much to avoid looking at her as to cement the layout in my head. As I gazed around the room, I realized how difficult it would have been to gain access, steal the object in question, and escape without ever being seen. It seemed impossible. Of course, the alternative was that it simply vanished into thin air. But after what I'd seen two months ago, I wasn't about to rule anything out yet. Suddenly, my headache came back with a vengeance.

"Is there anything else you'd like to see?" Dr. Halgrave asked.

"Not at the moment," I told her through clenched teeth. I took a deep breath and blew it out slowly. "I'll take the case. Brenda will send you the paperwork and I'll get started. I'd like to see all the security footage from that day if possible."

"Oh good," Halgrave sighed. "I was worried that after seeing the video you wouldn't."

"I'm not guaranteeing anything other than I'll look into it. Right now, I'm clueless."

"So are we, Mason. So are we."

"I'm sorry. Tell me again what this artifact is," I said.

We were back in Dr. Halgrave's office. She'd already briefly described it, but I was having trouble focusing again. This time I blamed it on the lobsters clawing their way through my skull.

She had to have been annoyed at having to repeat herself. Lord knows I would have been, but she patiently explained it again. "It is a medium sized figurine that we believe represents the ancient god Baal. It was recovered from a site in Syria last month. With the political instability and fundamentalist activity, recovering anything from that region is extremely difficult. It's also imperative that we try to save everything we can before it is destroyed."

"Right. Is there any reason someone would want to steal this particular item? Is it more valuable than the others surrounding it?"

"Not really. It's valuable, certainly; most three thousand-year-old artifacts are. But as far as anyone knows, it has no extraordinary significance or value. That's one of the puzzling aspects. Why take this? I should think anyone skilled enough to pull off a theft like this would choose something far more prestigious."

"Would it be easy to sell? On the black market?" I asked.

"Probably. There is an established network of smuggling operations that fund terrorist groups in the region, which is one of the reasons procuring legitimate items is so difficult. Most of the highly sought-after items, however, have connections to the Christian or Islamic religions. This particular relic predates those, but is so obscure in nature, few people would be aware of its value."

"It wasn't random, then. At least not in terms of selling. Guess I need to do some research, find out if another private collector has been rounding up similar items." I paused and met her gaze but held it for only a second. "I like to work multiple angles on a case."

"Of course," she said with a hint of a smile on her lips. When we made eye contact, I felt dizzy, like I was losing my balance. What the hell was going on? I needed to get out of here and clear my head.

We'd already watched the video of my "experiment" and it wasn't promising. The attempts to conceal myself behind the shelving unit hadn't worked. There were simply too many openings to be completely invisible. Obscured, sure, but to be completely unseen just wasn't possible that I could tell. We finished up our business and she escorted me back to the east entrance.

4

It had only taken an hour to meet with Dr. Halgrave. I was tempted to find some dark hole to crawl into and sleep off the headache, but once I was out of the building, it began to ease, so I decided to knock a couple of other things off my to-do list. I wanted to have a sit down with Cleve and pick his brain, find out if he remembered anything out of the ordinary from the day the artifact disappeared, but he wasn't available yet and I wanted a chance to look at the rest of the security footage first. Instead, I figured I'd clock out and work on my personal vendetta against the CPD. I pulled the Buick onto Lake Shore Drive heading south.

Smitty's was a tiny little neighborhood bar on the near south side. A lot of similar places don't open until late afternoon, so I wasn't even sure if it would be open, but it was worth a shot. I drove around the block a couple of times until I found a parking spot and then walked up to the door. Neon ads for Old Style and High Life hung in the tiny windows along with posters for music groups and small theatre companies, all but blocking the view. Turned out they were open for lunch. That was good. I was hungry.

Inside, cherry wood paneling covered the walls. Once it would have been lavish—a warm, inviting place to have a cocktail while listening to Dizzy Gillespie bebop and scat through the evening. Now, however, the charm had faded with age, and decades of nicotine residue had built up on the wood giving it a dingy appearance.

The room was long and narrow, with just enough space for several small tables arranged in a line that ran parallel to the bar itself. Two other gentlemen sat on barstools, chowing down on a pub burger. I settled myself on a stool close to the entrance, and the bartender ambled over to take my order. He appeared to be around my age, late thirties or early forties, head shaved to a silky finish, most likely to hide the onset of male pattern baldness.

"Haven't seen you in here before," he said, leaning on the bar.

"Never been here before," I replied.

"What can I get you?"

I ordered a burger and fries. They had a small kitchen in the back to prepare the typical pub fare—nothing fancy. This struck me as the kind of place you were supposed to order a beer with your meal, but I've never been much for beer, so I got a gin and tonic.

"What brings you in?" he asked after punching the order into a small computer.

"I was in the neighborhood on business and thought I'd pop in."

"What do you do?" It was a simple question; just the proprietor making small talk while he made my drink. I could have lied and told him anything. After all, I was here for information about a patron and didn't want to put him off, but instead, I told him the truth.

"Private eye," I said. "I'm working a case in the neighborhood. I like to try out the local places when I can. Plus, I heard you get some cops in here. Cops know all the good places."

"Well, we get a few regulars in here, but I wouldn't go around saying we're a cop bar or anything." He placed the drink on a napkin in front of me and smiled, but there was also a hint of warning in his voice like he was glad for the compliment but wary of getting a reputation that could be a double-edged sword.

"Nah, I didn't mean it like that. Just heard the place mentioned by a detective, Conrad, over at Second District. You know him?"

The bartender looked thoughtful for a moment, then said, "Think so. Red-haired fella?"

"Kind of. Wouldn't call him a ginger, though."

The bartender laughed at that. "No, I wouldn't either."

"He come in here a lot?"

"Every Thursday. He plays darts with a couple other guys. Don't think they're cops though."

"Even cops have lives outside the job," I reminded him.

I had the information I wanted. It was Wednesday.

I'd be coming back tomorrow to see if I could "bump into" Conrad and have a little conversation.

When the food arrived, I tucked in. It was pretty good grub. I gave my compliments to the chef and left a nice tip for the bartender. Had to make sure I was welcome next time.

***

I got back to the office mid-afternoon. I parked the Buick and went up the back way as usual. Willy was waiting for me, as usual, asking to be let in. His pleas to be let inside were growing more insistent. I briefly considered it but wasn't sure how Brenda would feel about having the stray inside, so I nudged him out of the way before entering.

Brenda stuck her head into the hallway as I walked by. "So?" she asked.

"We got the job," I said.

"Great! I'll get started on the paperwork. By the way, a package came for you a little while ago. It's in your office."

"Thanks."

While Brenda got started on the paperwork, I found the package lying on the brown leather couch in my office. It was sealed in a nondescript cardboard box and felt substantial, so I sliced through the packing tape with my pocket knife and looked inside. It contained an external hard drive. I figured it was the surveillance footage I had requested. I was impressed how quickly they'd gotten it together. Of course, I suspected they'd already done so for the police and simply had to make a copy for me.

Hooking the hard drive up to my desktop and opening the files, I saw there were a dozen folders labeled numerically, and it took me a few minutes to determine that each folder corresponded to a different camera. It took me even longer to identify the camera that captured the mysterious disappearance. I watched the footage that I'd already seen at the museum but didn't pick up on anything different.

Next, I went through the video from the other cameras and was eventually able to piece together a mental map of their position from my brief tour of the storage facility. Each view overlapped slightly with that of the adjacent camera, though every other one displayed a view from the opposite wall. The only blind spots were directly under each camera. However, because of the staggered positioning on opposite walls, it would have been impossible to move from one blind spot to the other without being visible. It was an excellent security design that provided more than adequate visual coverage. It also left me more baffled than before. I had absolutely no idea how the thief had managed to swipe the artifact and avoid detection unless the footage had somehow been tampered with.

I picked up the phone and dialed my go-to computer guru. I didn't know if he had any experience analyzing video footage, but it wouldn't hurt to ask.

"Computer 911. If you've got a problem, I've got a solution." Mac always did sound chipper.

"Don't you have caller id? You don't have to say that every time I call."

"Sure I do. It's in the manual. Just ask HR."

"HR?" I started, frustration creeping into my voice. Then I realized that's what he was going for, so I grumbled, "Fine, I'll file a complaint later."

Mac chuckled at that. "What can I do for you, Gray?"

Mac ran a one-man PC fix-it shop. He was a genius with all things computer related. He'd been invaluable in bringing down the real estate firm Brenda had worked for.

"You know anything about digital video? Like how to tell if footage has been tampered with?"

"Video, huh? I did a little editing back in college, but that's been a few years. It's not really in my wheelhouse, but I might know a guy." There was a brief pause as he looked through his contacts. "Yeah, here it is. Eddie Vallard. He's got his own studio and does lots of editing and production. I heard he does consults for the police from time to time." He gave me the number and I wrote it down. "Anything else?"

"Nah, that's it. Thanks. I'll let you know."

"No problem," he said, and we hung up.

I dialed the number for Eddie Vallard and, after explaining who I was and what I wanted to both the receptionist and his assistant, I was finally transferred to the man himself.

Once again, I explained that I was a private investigator interested in finding out if some video footage had been tampered with.

"Yeah, I can do that, but my schedule is kinda full right now." Eddie sounded young and very laid back. "Might be able to squeeze you in next week if it's important."

"I was hoping for something a little sooner. Do you know anybody else that could look at it today or tomorrow?"

"Sorry. If I did, I'd pass it along. I'd love to share the wealth. Not that there's much money in what you're asking. It's usually the cops that need my services. I'm registered with the forensic science department, you know, but they don't pay a lot. I spent a whole day going over some video from a museum yesterday and they gave me a lousy five hundred bucks."

"Wait," I interrupted. "The Field Museum?"

"Yeah, why?"

"That's what I have. You already looked at it?"

"I'm not supposed to talk about it, but yeah. I

looked at it," he admitted. "Freaky shit. I could see why they wanted me."

"An artifact seems to disappear into thin air...yeah, I'd call that freaky. So what did you find? Had anything been deleted?"

"I didn't find a damn thing. As far as I could tell, nothing was missing. The feed hadn't been compromised at all. The whole thing was clean."

"Damn...I was really hoping for something. All right, thanks, Eddie. I'll keep your number if you don't mind."

"Sure thing," he said and hung up.

Since that was a dead end, I turned my attention back to the computer. I spent the next several hours combing through the surveillance, looking for anything out of the ordinary. It was frustrating. I'd done my share of watching video like this before. It's a long, arduous process. Most of it is incredibly boring, but you can't zone out because you might miss something important. When Brenda left at five, I still had nada.

There were twelve hours of footage from each of the dozen cameras. I didn't have time to watch it all, so I focused on the half-hour block of time preceding the dis-appearance. By eight o'clock I had watched it all, seen nothing suspicious, and my head was pounding.

I got up and took a couple of ibuprofen, made a pot of coffee, and went out to the balcony for a cigarette. I was hoping the combination of cold air, caffeine, and nicotine would get me through another hour or two and stave off the lobsters.

Willy sat next to his empty bowl staring off into the darkness. He turned his head when I stepped outside but said nothing. I joined him at the railing and stared out at the night too.

There's not much of a view from our back balcony. You can't see the skyline or anything, but there's a couple of trees and a small courtyard between us and the next building, with a nice patch of sky above. It's peaceful.

I lit my cigarette, took a long drag, and blew it out heavily.

"I don't know, Willy," I said to the cat. "This one's got me stumped. How does something like that just vanish into thin air? It can't, right?" Willy flicked an ear but still didn't say anything. "Right...just like vampires can't exist." This time he did look at me, albeit with a bored expression, and licked his whiskers.

"Back to square one, then. Look at the evidence again but through a different lens. I can do that." I finished my smoke and dropped the butt in a jar I keep out there for that purpose. I might poison my own lungs, but there's no sense in mucking up the neighborhood if I can help it. I took another sip of coffee, which was cooling off rapidly and turned to go back inside.

Before I could take a step, Willy wound between

my legs and plopped his haunches right in front of the door, glaring at me.

"Insistent little bastard, aren't you? Fine, you can come in for a while. I owe you that much, I guess."

Once inside, Willy sauntered through the kitchenette like he owned the place, sparing the tiniest of glances at his surroundings and proceeded down the hallway toward my office. I followed, curious to see what he thought of the place. He didn't pause or roam around exploring. Rather, he walked directly to the brown leather couch and sprung onto the back in one leap. There he settled himself down and turned only his head to watch me.

"Make yourself at home, why don't you," I told him. He flicked his tail.

I snorted and went back to the computer. I decided to go back to the original shot. This time I cued it up right as Cleve entered the picture and advanced it one frame at a time, watching him closely. From the angles I judged earlier, I doubted he had swiped the little statue, but the fact that it vanished just as he passed between it and the camera was too coincidental to be ignored.

I almost missed it.

I had, in fact, missed the anomaly every other time I'd watched it. It was only visible in a single frame, not nearly long enough to pick up on in real time.

What I saw was an odd shape extending from

Cleve's shoulder, or maybe protruding from behind it. It was dark, blending in with the guard's own jacket. It could have been mistaken for a bunching of the fabric that stuck out at a strange angle, but the blazer showed no sign of riding up or sitting askew. It could have been a shadow cast from some other object, perhaps on a shelf above, but there had been no flicker of light and the brevity of its duration made me doubt that was its cause.

I leaned back in my chair with no idea what this anomaly actually was. But it was something.

With this discovery came a fresh wave of skull grinding, eye piercing pain. I almost fell backwards out the chair when it hit with the force of a sledgehammer. Bursts of non-existent light blinded me. If I could just lie down and close my eyes, everything would be okay. I staggered to my feet and stumbled the three steps over to the couch where I flopped down on it, too drained to do anything else. Willy watched with mild curiosity.

I lay there for what seemed like hours, waiting for the throbbing to subside. It didn't. It got worse. The throbbing turned to pounding like a symphony of rail-road picks slamming into quarried stone. Eyes closed, I let darkness envelop me, but it did nothing to ease the agony. I was caught in a standing wave of pain, my ears full of the roaring locomotive sound of a tornado. This is how I would die, I thought. Alone in my head, cut off from those I cared about. Maybe it would be a relief, a sudden silence from the onslaught. But what if it wasn't? What if this was a glimpse into the torment of Hell? That scared me more than anything.

Then, through the blackness and the incessant roar came a voice.

Can you hear me, boy?

The voice was a rich baritone, textured with a layer of rough authority and edged with impatience that reminded me of my father. It was faint, distant.

My eyelids were heavy, but I opened them just enough to peer through slits. It was like trying to see through a cyclone, a swirling mass of dust and darkness.

Boy? said the voice again. It came from the other side.

I hear you, I thought.

Good. It's not too late then. Let me in. We have important things to discuss. Yeah, he sounded just like my old man.

Pop, is that you?

No, boy, I just want to help.

I'm dying.

Yes, but I can help.

How?

Let me in.

I didn't know what he meant. How could I let someone into a storm? The voice seemed much closer now. Almost as if I could reach out and touch it. So, I did.

I extended my arm into the swirling clouds, reaching through them, clawing at the gloom. A hand grasped mine from the other side. With my last ounce of strength, I heaved, pulling the speaker toward me. Slowly, a silhouette materialized in the haze and stepped close, placing a heavy, knotted hand on my shoulder.

The world fell away. The storm, the swirling winds, the relentless rumble. The pain. It all vanished instantly.

5

The hand released my shoulder and I heard footsteps retreat into the darkness. I opened my eyes all the way.

A weathered man, perhaps in his late fifties, reclined against my desk, arms crossed in front of a burly chest. He wore a slate-colored suit, a style from days gone by, the cuffs starting to fray. A pocked and heavily lined face was framed by a thick grizzled beard. Most striking was the long scar that ran from forehead to jaw, the old wound having obliterated his left eye, leaving a blank and shriveled socket behind.

"Cut that one close," he said. "Thought we might lose you."

"What happened? Where am I?"

"You're in your office, boy. Sort of."

"What do you mean, sort of?" I asked, not sure what to make of this strange man.

"I won't lie to you, boy. You don't have time for games, and you'd figure it out eventually, I imagine. This is your office as you remember it, as it exists in your mind. You're dreaming."

"Dreaming?"

"Aye. I don't have time to explain everything. Not if you want to survive the night, so listen up.

"Your headaches are being caused by the barrage

of energy bombarding your psyche." He said it so matter-of-factly that it left little room for doubt. "If you don't learn to protect yourself, it'll burn you up from the inside and leave your withered husk behind."

Just because he sounded convincing didn't mean I knew what the hell he was talking about, so I said, "What the hell are you talking about?"

He sighed. "Two months ago, you stepped into a world few men know about, let alone ever see. You touched energies that your brightest scientists haven't even begun to explore."

The dreams came back to me then, with vivid clarity, and suddenly I was no longer in my office, but floating above the city. Below were the strange lights coursing through the streets.

"Ah, is this what they look like to you? Interesting." The old man was floating beside me. "This energy," he said gesturing to the writhing lights "responded when you first touched it, correct?"

"Yeah," I said, remembering how they'd recoiled at first, then flowed into my hands.

"You're a conduit. It's drawn to you now. It wants to flow through you like electricity through a lightning rod."

"That's a bad thing, right?"

He looked at me and his brow crinkled. "Ever see what happens to someone that sticks a fork in an electrical outlet?"

I hadn't, but the point was made. "So why didn't I get fried the first time? Or the second?"

"You used it, didn't you?

"Maybe," I admitted. "I'm still not sure what happened exactly."

"What do you think happened?"

"I think the blue lights helped me heal. The red ones made me angry but gave me strength."

"Good." He paused, gathering his thoughts. "This energy, though it is different from other forms, follows a set of laws like the rest. Like electricity or heat, when harnessed and handled properly in small amounts, it can be used without posing much danger."

The city below dissolved before my eyes and suddenly we were sitting in the middle of a dank cave, peering out into a snowstorm, a campfire blazing at our feet.

"When mankind first learned how to manage fire, he was able to stay warm on cold nights and improve his diet by cooking food." He paused, but when I said nothing, continued. "Before man learned to control it, fire was a thing to be feared. Imagine if your only experience with it was when a wall of heat came roaring toward you through the forest or prairie, burning everything it touched. Electricity has a similar story. With the discoveries of Franklin, Edison, and Faraday, it became commonplace, though no less dangerous if uncontrolled."

"So you think I can control these lights?" I asked, staring at the icy flakes swirling beyond the mouth of the cave.

"I do."

"How?"

"That, I can't tell you. I know it can be done. I've seen it done before. But how? That's outside my realm of expertise."

"Can't I just leave it alone? Ignore it? If you don't play with fire, you won't get burned, right?"

"Turning your back on a raging inferno will not prevent you from being incinerated," he replied.

The fire at my feet flickered, casting a wavering shadow on the wall. Could this man be telling the truth? I still didn't know who he was, or if he was even real. If this was a dream, the whole conversation was probably just an invention of my addled brain, brought on by the headaches themselves.

"I know all of this is sudden," spoke the old man once more. "Would that I had been able to reach you earlier, to prepare you for this new reality that you are trying so hard to pretend doesn't exist."

"You still haven't told me who you are."

"Ah. Survive the night, and we will speak more about that. I will warn you that when I leave, the storm will return. It's not going to be easy, and if you don't deal with it now, you will die."

I looked again at my shadow dancing on the rough stone wall. A thought surfaced. What was more real: the shadow or the man casting it? If the shadow was all that I had ever seen—if I had never before encountered my own reflection in a mirror—would that shadow be the entirety of my reality? Would I even consider the possibility that I might appear otherwise? How then, might I feel upon encountering my true reflection for the first time? As puzzled and skeptical as I felt now?

"Good luck," said the old man, and he faded from sight. My task was clear. I must turn from the shadows and seek out their source. With this new determination, the cave faded from existence and I was plunged into complete blackness. The dull roar of the storm returned, and I knew I had only moments before it consumed me.

Focusing my thoughts, I called up images of the blue and red energy from the ballroom at Navy Pier. There I had seen them in tandem with my surroundings, not in a dream. I fixed part of my mind on that image and with another part I thought of myself lying prone on the couch in my office.

The vision that sprang to life before me was blinding in its intensity. Waves of the mysterious energy poured through the windows of the office, writhing around my sleeping form, lashing out with violent tendrils of light, stabbing into my eyes, furling themselves around my limbs. All of this I saw as I hovered just above myself. To call it surreal was an understatement.

This was the psychic barrage the old man warned me about.

How could I stop it?

My mind raced furiously, trying to sort it all out. He said this was energy like any other that followed rules and could be manipulated. He compared it to fire. Maybe I could insulate myself from it like firemen did with their protective coats. But what would I use? If it was my mind that was being pummeled, maybe a mental barrier was needed. How to build it? Without knowledge or an understanding of the nature of this energy, I would have to rely on intuition.

In my years as an investigator, both on the force and as an independent, intuition had helped me solve just as many puzzles as reason and intellect. Reason is the process of drawing a conclusion with the conscious mind and being fully aware of evidence and assumptions. Intuition is a process of the subconscious, drawing conclusions without being aware of all the pieces. Some dismiss the process, but I believe it is no less valid than the other.

I closed my mind's eye to the sight below and turned my attention inward, imagining a wall constructed of mental force surrounding me. At first, there was no substance to it, so I concentrated even harder, willing it into existence. Immediately, the force of the attack lessened. I opened my eyes again and saw why. The serpentine cords lashed no less furiously, but they were being blocked by the wall. As I watched, however, my shield was being torn apart, or perhaps burned away. It was difficult to tell which. It would not hold for long though, and I was mentally drained. That was not the way.

During the brief respite, I thought about the other analogy: electricity. How was one protected from that? Insulators, similar to the shield I tried. But there was something else. An idea began to form. If I couldn't block the energy, perhaps I could redirect it. No amount of insulation could protect someone from a lightning strike. Instead, the lightning was routed around people and buildings using a lightning rod. Could I make something like that? A psychic faraday cage, perhaps? It was worth a try.

I turned my focus inward once more, searching for something to build with. Willpower wouldn't work for this. It was too ephemeral. Something more permanent was needed: a durable conduit to channel the bulk of the energy around my psyche harmlessly.

This is where my explanation for what happened gets a bit ticklish. My understanding, I feel, is too limited for an accurate description. Considering the effects these lights had had on me in the past, I believed the substance they sought out within me to be part of my emotional makeup, or perhaps my very essence.

I know myself well. It's one of the perks of the copious amounts of quiet introspection and self-reflection that comes with my job--and lone wolf status. This allowed me to do a little soul searching quickly, finding what I was looking for: a thread of my own life force. I needed an anchor point, a place to "ground" my little lightning rod.

All of this was connected to my dreams somehow. The first one came after I'd been attacked by a vampire. It had been a mish-mash of images, making little sense. But one had appeared in later dreams and seemed significant: a mirror. A mirror that reflected an eerie, other-worldly Chicago, colored in hues of gray. It seemed right.

Conjuring the image of that mirror, I looped the strand of my own "ness" around it and carefully threaded it through the glass and into the misty reflection beyond. Next, I wrapped the other end around myself and fashioned a little spike at the top of my head. If I was going for lightning rod, I might as well go all out.

When my little project was complete, I stepped out of myself to see what I'd accomplished. The pounding surf of glowing energy was gone. In its place was more of a river, streams of light flowing lazily and harmlessly through my construct. I eyed it for a while, watching to see if things would erode like the first shield I'd put up, but it appeared stable. At least for now.

My headache was gone.

It worked. I hadn't the faintest notion of what I'd

actually done, which disturbed me at first, but then decided I should focus on the accomplishment and try to figure out the logistics later.

That's when I realized how exhausted I was. More than just tired, a marrow-deep weariness had crept into my body, and I didn't think I could stay awake any longer. Except I was already asleep, wasn't I? The whole night was confusing. I longed for the deep black of true slumber. Thankfully, my wish was granted.

6

Golden fingers of dawn, reaching through the slatted window blinds, crept across the floor when I awoke. All was silent. My head still didn't hurt. I peeled my face off the brown leather and sat up.

Willy lay on the back of the sofa breathing shallowly. His eye cracked open as I looked at him and he flicked an ear.

Looking at my watch, I determined I still had half an hour before Brenda arrived. Silently, I made a pot of coffee and stepped onto the balcony for a cigarette. Willy stayed where he was.

It was freezing—the kind of morning when everything is too cold to move, as if the air itself resists even the vibration of sound. My brain enjoyed the silence of both sound and thought. I tried not to disturb the tranquility. Usually, I would be thinking of a hundred things that needed to be done, but surprisingly, this morning I didn't have that problem. I enjoyed the rest of my smoke and went back inside.

It had been three days since I'd been home, and a sponge bath wasn't going to cut it today. I needed a shower.

Pouring coffee into a paper cup, I left the pot on for Brenda then bundled myself up to prepare for the frigid car. As I headed for the door, Willy stretched himself and yawned, poking his claws into the vinyl a time or two, then dropped to the floor and casually slipped outside with me.

When I got to the car and opened the driver's side door, he hopped in and plopped himself into the passenger seat. I paused for the briefest of moments, considering whether I should shoo him out before shrugging and crawling in the car myself.

It took a few minutes for the old Buick to warm up, but once it did, I loosened up my coat and settled into the drive home. Willy appeared to be napping again. By the time we reached Edgewater, street parking was plentiful, so I docked the boat one street back from my apartment and killed the engine.

"I guess you'll want to come in," I said to Willy without looking at him. He didn't answer. I popped the latch on the door and swung my legs out into the street. Willy waited until I had mostly extracted myself, then oozed out himself. There was something unusual about the way he moved. He didn't slink or skulk like some cats. He wasn't stealthy—that would imply an intent to remain hidden. Nor did he lightly leap and cavort—that would be too dainty. Yet there was a kind of grace to his walk. I mulled this over, searching for the right word to describe it as we walked the block to the back steps. The only thing I'd come up with by the time I was unlocking the door was "lithe efficiency" but that still wasn't quite right.

Willy waited patiently and actually let me enter first. I left him to his own devices while I made a phone call.

"Dr. Halgrave?" I said when she picked up. "It's Gray. I need to meet with Cleve today."

"Mason? I'm glad to hear from you. And please, call me Meredith."

"Of course."

"Have you found something?"

"Maybe. I'm not sure," I told her. "I don't want to get your hopes up this soon, but if it turns into something, you'll be the first to know."

"Alright. I'll see you when you get here," she said.

"Uh, actually," I cut in before she could hang up. "It would probably be better if you didn't sit in on this. I want him as comfortable as possible and that might be difficult if you're there." Which was true. I would also be very uncomfortable with her there, but I wasn't going to tell her that.

"Ohhkay," she said hesitantly. "I guess I can understand that. I would appreciate it if you'd check in with me before you left, though."

"Of course." That placated her, so we got off the phone.

Next, I turned my attention to getting cleaned up. I stripped down and tossed my grungy clothes into the hamper. After so long without a shower, a good scalding was in order.

As the water rinsed away old tensions, my mind picked at the discoveries I'd recently made, trying to unravel them like a knotted ball of kite string. Foremost was last night's dream, if that's what it was. Most dreams fade quickly after waking, and those that linger become fuzzy, with only a few details remaining intact. My memories from last night, however, were quite vivid.

Also present was the shadow I'd seen in the security footage. What could have made it? If it was a person concealing themselves or using another ordinary misdirection, I should be able to find some other evidence. Perhaps Cleve had seen something that he hadn't realized was significant. In my current state of mind, however, I couldn't help but wonder if something beyond ordinary was responsible.

After showering and shaving, I walked into the living room with my towel wrapped around me. Willy was perched on the back of the couch. I stared at him for a moment. Hard. Reaching a decision, I continued to the bedroom and got dressed.

I emerged a new man. Well, at least a clean, presentable version of my old self.

"Don't piss on anything," I told the cat as I pulled on coat, hat, and gloves then locked up the apartment and hiked to the Red Line.

***

Between the train schedule, the bus transfer, and walking across the campus, I arrived at the museum a little before noon. Roger let me through security without any hassle and radioed Cleve. He was headed to the on-site cafe for lunch but said over the radio that I could meet him there.

The cafe wasn't terribly crowded. As I said, weekdays in the winter aren't the busiest times for tourists, and there weren't any school groups camping out for lunch. I spotted Cleve quickly. After all, I had spent several hours watching him walk across my computer screen. He gave me a wary smile as I approached.

"Afternoon, Cleve," I said as I offered him my hand. "Glad to meet you."

He accepted the handshake. Cleve appeared pretty average in all ways. Average height, average build. Which is to say he was about five-nine and a little overweight. He looked to be in his early fifties and wore black pants with a black button-down uniform shirt. The only remarkable thing about him was his face. He had big, exaggerated features that made him look friendly, if not a little comedic.

"What can I get you for lunch?" I asked.

He squinted at me and sucked his teeth. "I got me a ham sandwich in the back."

"I know you've already been through the wringer with the cops and I hate to take up more of your time, so lunch is the least I can do," I told him.

"Well...I'd hate to hurt a man's feelings by turning down an offer like that." He grinned. "Italian beef is pretty good here." It was a long "I", like "Eye-tal-ian". "It ain't Al's by half, but it'll do. Side of fries and a pop, too."

I laughed and went to the counter to order. Figuring Cleve knew what was decent, I followed his lead and ordered two sandwiches, giardiniera on the side, and delivered the steaming plates as soon as they were ready. We made small talk while we ate, and I let him get through half the beef before turning the conversation in a more serious direction.

"I'm sure you've been over this a hundred times already with the cops, but I need to ask you a few questions."

"Don't know as I can tell you anything different," he said, "but we can have another go."

"First, let me say I don't think you had anything to do with it. But I saw something...odd on the video, something I can't explain. I'm hoping you can. Or at least get me pointed in the right direction."

"See what I can do."

"Great. You have a regular route you patrol?"

"Yep," he said between bites.

"You do the same route two or three times a day?"

"Huh-uh," he shook his head. "One big one. Covers the same areas a couple times, though."

Well, that was good. It showed that Cleve wasn't just going through the motions with his security job. He didn't want to be too predictable in his route which meant he was probably still pretty observant on duty. Maybe he would be helpful.

"I want you to show me." His eyebrows rose at that and he put down his sandwich. "No rush. Finish eating first," I told him. He nodded and tucked in.

Twenty minutes later he was leading me in a large figure eight through the ground floor. We passed through the Ancient Egypt exhibit and were heading toward the Underground Adventure. I hadn't expected such a thorough tour.

"I'm really interested in your route through the Resource Center," I said, hoping to speed things up a bit.

"Oh, right." Our path straightened out and he made for the elevators.

Once again, I found myself in the long, brightly-lit hallway that was the only way in or out of the Resource Center. Whoever had taken the artifact had to have come through here. I guess I'd be looking through that footage again later. As we passed by the security checkpoint, I had a thought.

"Actually, Cleve, I just had an idea. Let's start where you leave and work backwards."

Cleve paused in his stride. "Okay, well, I leave the same way we came in so..."

We pushed through the doors into the next hallway and he veered to the first door on the right. Once inside the main storage room, he slowed. Walking a routine backwards takes some thought. We went up and down several rows of shelves while I kept my eye on where the artifact had been.

"Have there been any thefts from here before this?" I asked.

He eyed me, then shrugged and said, "Not in a long time, I think. With security as tight as it is, I still can't figure how they got this one. Before all the high-tech gear, there were a few. Most got caught, though."

We made our way back toward what I'd come to think of as the Main Aisle and turned to walk its length. We passed the missing artifact's spot and kept going. Cleve walked smack down the middle of the aisle. There was plenty of space for someone to walk next to him.

After a sweep through the cavernous room, he left through the far door and went back into the main hall. We passed the numerous doors leading to various labs and moved back toward the exit. I stopped him halfway down.

I turned my attention to the ceiling, looking for cameras. I didn't see any. Which was strange. With all the coverage of the facility, why were there no cameras in this hallway?

"Cleve, there any cameras here?"

"Huh? No." He paused. "Not that I know of."

I kept scrutinizing the walls, paying close attention to the line where the wall met the ceiling. And then I saw it. A tiny black dot.

I pointed to the spot. "Cleve, what's that?"

He squinted up to where I was pointing. "Don't know."

"I think it's a camera," I said.

"Really?"

"I think so. If it is, I wasn't sent any footage from it. Can we look into that?"

"Probably," he said. "I'll need to check with the boss."

A short radio conversation and brisk walk later, we were sitting in a small office that housed a number of servers. It was the security and surveillance nerve center. A sweaty guy named John looked nervously between me and Cleve.

"It just got installed the other day. It's not supposed to be online yet. Apparently, there were issues with the wireless signal in that hallway," the guy said.

"Okay, well, is there any chance it's online now?"

"Maybe." He just sat there staring at us.

"So, check already," I said, irritation coloring my tone.

"Oh, right," said John as he swiveled in his chair and pecked on the keyboard. After a minute, he sat back and said, "Huh."

"What?" I asked.

"Well, it looks like that camera is working and it has been for a while. The technicians said they'd let me know when they had the network in order, but they never did, so I just assumed it wasn't working yet."

"Does that mean there's footage on your server from that night that no one has seen yet?"

"Yeah, I guess it does."

I had him focus on the day of the theft. The screen displayed a long shot of the hallway from a high angle. We scanned the video quickly, watching for anyone who seemed out of place. People zipped by; some went in and out of various doors. I spotted Cleve streaking across the screen and had him pause it.

"How many times a day do you check the storage area?"

"Twice."

I nodded, then had him continue the scan.

The time code in the top right-hand corner was speeding closer to the time of the theft.

"Slow it down," I instructed.

A figure walked into one of the labs, closing the door behind him. Several minutes went by with no other activity, then Cleve slid past again. After that, it was quiet for a long time. Eventually, Cleve walked back down the hallway. The timestamp told me the disappearance had already occurred. I stood there staring at the empty hall-way without a clue. That's when I noticed the door to the lab stood slightly ajar.

"Stop." I pointed to the screen. "Look at that. Someone went in there and closed the door behind them. Now it's open a crack, but I never saw anyone come out." I looked at Cleve who blinked back at me. Then to the technician I said, "Back it up." He did.

I let it run until the mysterious figure came out of the room backwards. "Stop it here." The image froze just as the person of interest was reaching for the door han-dle. No one else was in the hallway. "Can you zoom in?" The tech punched a few buttons and the frame tightened on the figure. It was a man. I was pretty sure of that. His back was to the camera. He wore a dark ball cap and a windbreaker. I couldn't see a face. Damn.

"Any idea who that is?" I asked both of them.

They shrugged.

"Okay, run it back slowly. Let's see if we can get a glimpse of his face."

We ran the video back until the stranger disap-peared from frame. At no time was there ever a clear shot of his face.

My phone buzzed. I took it out of my pocket and saw it was Nancy.

"Give me a second, fellas," I said as I thumbed it on. "Hey Nancy, what's up?"

"Earl, it's about Maggie." Nancy's voice was strained.

I felt a spike of fear and stepped out into the hallway.

"What's wrong?"

"I think her arm is broken. The school called and said she had an accident in gym class. She's clutching it, crying, and won't let anybody touch it. She's refusing to leave because I might take her to the hospital. I don't know what to do, Earl." Nancy's the only one that calls me Earl. It's my first name, and I hate it. But coming from her, it just sounds right.

"Let me talk to her." There was a pause, and I imagined Nancy holding the phone up to her daughter's ear.

"Hello?" squeaked a tiny voice.

"Hey Bumble Bee. I heard you had an accident at school." I kept my voice calm, soothing.

"It wasn't an accident. Christian kicked me on purpose."

"Did he now?"

"Uh huh," she whimpered.

"Arm hurts pretty bad, huh?"

"Yeah."

"Hospitals, though. They're scary places."

"Bad things happen there," she whispered.

"You know I have a history with hospitals, right?

Twice last year. Nothing bad happened to me. In fact, they did a pretty good job of fixing my ugly face." She didn't respond. "Tell you what, kiddo. How about I meet you there? We can face the scary together."

"Promise?" she mumbled.

"Cross my heart," I promised.

"Okay," she sniffled.

"Okay."

7

Maggie was four when Frank and Nancy pulled me from the gutter and helped put my life back together. That year for Halloween, she dressed up as a bumble bee. It was the perfect costume for her. She was a cute little girl that begged to be cuddled, but she also had quite a temper and her words could sting even the toughest old man like me. Ever since, I had called her Bumble Bee.

As much as I cared for Nancy and Alice, I had a ridiculous soft spot for Maggie.

Waiting for a cab outside the museum was torture. I'd asked Cleve to let Dr. Halgrave know I had a personal matter come up and hustled outside. I couldn't get to the hospital fast enough.

It cost a pretty penny, but we made good time, and I rolled out the door as soon as we pulled up to the emergency room entrance and dashed inside.

Both Nancy and Maggie sat in the waiting room. Maggie still clutched her arm and was shaking her head stubbornly as a triage nurse tried to convince her to go in the back. When they saw me, Nancy's face brightened while Maggie scowled at the nurse and said, "Not without him."

I scooped her up and told the nurse to lead the way, Nancy trailing behind. I sat with her while they took the x-rays, draped with a lead vest, chatting about what happened.

"We were playing basketball," she told me, "The ball was rolling across the floor, so I was going to pick it up and pass it to Amanda, but Christian ran over and tried to kick it. He missed and kicked me in the arm."

"Ouch," I said, cringing.

"Who kicks a basketball? That's not how you play. Everybody knows that. So, I punched him."

"You punched him?" I sounded shocked, but it didn't surprise me.

"He deserved it."

"Maybe. Did you get in trouble?"

"No. Maybe. Mom yelled at the principal."

I chuckled. "Really? I bet that was something. I don't think I've ever heard her yell."

"She yells at Alice all the time."

"Well, Alice is a teenager. Sometimes the only thing they hear is yelling."

"Yeah. Ow," she winced as the x-ray tech repositioned her arm for another picture.

"You know, I broke my arm once when I was a kid."

"You did? What happened?"

"My dad built me this treehouse. It was totally cool. I'd play in it for hours. One time, I found this old rope in the garage, and I thought it would make a great way to swing from the tree house to a big branch on the next tree over. So, I hauled it up onto the platform and threw it over a limb as high as I could and tied it. I was so excited. I thought I'd be like Tarzan or something. Well, I tried to swing across, but the rope broke. I found out later the rope was really old and half rotten."

"Did it hurt?"

"You bet. I cried like a baby." She looked mollified by that.

The tech said we were done and led us back to the exam room. We sat there making small talk while we waited for the doctor to show up. I'm not very good at small talk and my mouth ran out of words pretty quick. Maybe it was because being in the hospital reminded me of pain, but sitting there, my thoughts drifted to my headaches. I hadn't had one sneak up and sucker punch me in a while. It was a little strange. I'd gotten used to them, and in their absence, I could almost forget about what was causing them. Almost.

I didn't like where my thoughts were going, so I decided to talk about the case. You know, because I didn't want to think about weird stuff.

I'm not supposed to discuss the details of a case with anyone not directly involved because of the confidentiality clause in the contract, and usually, I don't breathe a word to anyone. But the nature of this one begged a fresh set of eyes. And kids are notorious for thinking outside the box.

"Let me ask you something, Bumble Bee. You might be able to help me with this case I've been working on." Her face lit up, so I continued. "Let's say there's this statue in a warehouse. The whole place is covered with cameras and security guards, but one day the statue just disappears. One second, it's there, the next...gone. Poof. No sign of anyone taking it. It just vanishes. What do you think happened to it?"

She looked thoughtful for a minute then asked, "How big?"

I held both hands up about a foot apart. "About like that."

"Well, from what you described," she said, putting on a serious face, "it could be one of two things." She was at that age where she was still mostly an innocent little girl but could sound like an adult when she tried. "Either someone invisible stole it or teleported it away."

"Teleported?" I wondered where she'd come up with that word.

"Yeah, that's kind of ridiculous. I don't think we've invented that yet."

"Guess that leaves invisible."

She nodded in agreement. Invisible, huh? After what I'd seen recently, I didn't dismiss it.

A doctor breezed into the room then, taking a second to smile at Maggie and introduce herself. "I'm Dr. Iasis. I'll be fixing you up today." It was the woman who saved me from the chef outside the restaurant. I'd never forget that face, though it didn't appear that she recognized me. She held an oversized envelope in one hand. From it, she withdrew several x-ray films and placed them on an illuminated board.

"So here's your arm," she said, "See this bone on the outside?" She ran her finger along the picture. "This is your ulna. If you look right here, you can see a little line. That's where it's broken. Luckily it isn't a bad break. All we have to do is put a cast on it and it will heal up on its own."

Nancy let out a breath she'd been holding and smiled at Maggie.

"So what happened?" Dr. Iasis asked.

"Stupid boy kicked me at school," Maggie told her.

"Ah. Stupid boys." The doctor winked at Maggie. "Well, let me get my supplies together, and we'll get you taken care of, okay." She turned and made eye contact with me, pausing for a brief second as if seeing me for the first time, then moved to gather the fiberglass wrap and bandages for making the cast.

Was that a glimmer of recognition?

We all watched in silence as Dr. Iasis prepared and molded the cast to Maggie's arm. It was a fairly quick process. As she got close to finishing, the doctor went through how to properly care for the cast. "The biggest thing to keep in mind is not to get it wet. If you take a shower, hang your arm out of the tub. But it's usually better and easier to just take a bath. It'll get sweaty and itchy after a while. It can't be helped, but don't try and scratch inside the cast with anything. Sometimes blowing air in it with a hairdryer helps." She finished applying the fiberglass before continuing. "There you go. Let's give it a couple minutes to set up, and we'll get you out of here. You'll come back in six weeks so we can remove it."

"Six weeks!" Maggie shrieked. "I have to wear this for six weeks?" She turned on her mother then. "What about the Christmas pageant? Angels don't wear casts!"

"Oh, honey, don't worry about that. I'll fix your costume up so no one will ever be able to tell," said Nancy in a soothing tone.

"I don't understand," Maggie shot back. "Uncle Gray was healed up in six days when he broke his jaw. Not six weeks."

Nancy and I shared a look, then I glanced at Dr. Iasis. We had her attention. "Six days?" she asked incredulously.

"Eh, it wasn't as broke as everybody claims," I told her, trying to brush Maggie's comment away. "That was a fluke, Mags. I think the doctors read the x-ray wrong," I lied. How could I explain what had actually happened? I couldn't. At least not here. Not now.

The doctor eyed me intently. I shrugged, not wanting to take the conversation any further.

"Have we met?" she finally asked.

I brightened immediately. "Actually, yeah. You saved my hide night before last. Outside of Moxy."

"Oh, right."

"Thanks again for that," I told her.

She nodded, then looked to Nancy. "I'm going to write a prescription for a painkiller. Her arm's going to ache for the next week, so she might need it to help her sleep. Hang tight while I make you a follow-up appointment and get that prescription." She looked me over once more and left the room.

Maggie was prodding at her new cast. Nancy reached out and took her hand, patting it gently and said, "See, that wasn't so bad, was it?"

"I guess not," admitted Maggie. "I still don't like hospitals, though."

I stood and walked over to them. "Me either," I agreed. "How about we both do our best to stay out of them from now on?"

Maggie smiled up at me. "Deal."

A few minutes later, Dr. Iasis returned with several papers stapled together: print-outs of how to care for the cast, the next appointment date, and a prescription. Nancy helped Maggie back into her sweater and coat—no easy task with the cast getting in the way—and thanked the doctor for her help.

Before we could leave, the doctor put a hand on

my arm.

"Your name is Gray, right?" she asked.

I nodded, thrilled she remembered.

"Do you have another card?"

"Sure," I said, digging into my wallet and handing her one. "That offer for coffee still stands, by the way."

She pocketed the card but didn't say anything else. She did, however, smile this time. And I fell in love just a little bit.

8

Cleve and the security tech had burned a DVD of the footage from the newly installed camera. I loaded it onto my computer when I got back to the office and queued it up to the mysterious visitor. I combed through it frame by frame, looking for something I may have missed earlier. I was able to find a shot of the guy that showed part of his face, but it was a bad angle with no way to identify him. I stared at it for a long time before realizing there was something else I hadn't seen. On the right arm of the jacket was an image or logo of some kind. I zoomed in as far as I could, hoping that the fancy new camera had a high enough definition to let me make out what it was, but I wasn't that lucky. The closer I zoomed in, the more pixelated it got. The image was just too small and too far away from the lens to see it with enough clarity. Frustrated, I captured a screenshot, then looked through footage from the other cameras once again. I couldn't find another shot of the guy anywhere.

Maggie had said an invisible person may have stolen the artifact. From what little evidence I could find, he might as well have been. The thief had clearly done his homework. He knew where all the security cameras were and had the skill to avoid them as well as escape notice by any people in the area. I didn't know how that was possible, but the fact that the new camera *had* caught him on tape told me it was.

If only I could figure out what that logo was.

I picked up the phone and punched in a number.

"May I speak with Mr. Vallard, please?" I asked the receptionist when she answered.

"Who's calling, please?"

"Detective Gray. I spoke with him yesterday and I have new information he might be interested in."

"One moment, please."

I held for five minutes before the line picked up again.

"Detective? This is Eddie. I hear you have some new information about that case. Did you find what you were looking for?"

"Sort of. Turns out there was some footage the cops never had access to."

"Really," he said, drawing the word out. I could tell he was curious. "Man, I'd love to process it for you, but like I said yesterday, I'm booked solid this week."

"No worries," I said. "I actually have a different question. I was able to pull an image of someone from it. Can't see the face, but there's a logo on the jacket that I can't make out. It's too pixelated when I zoom in. Is there any program I could get that could clean it up, fill in the holes?"

"Damn, yeah, but it's pricey. That's top of the line processing software. Hang on." There was a pause as he held the phone away and spoke to someone else. "Okay, I might be able to help you out. Something like that, I can get running in a few minutes. Software might take a while to render anything usable, though. Cost you fifty bucks."

"I can handle that. Want me to email it over?"

"Nah, that won't work. Burn me a copy of the footage, note the timestamp of the still you want processed and messenger it."

"Okay. I'll send it over shortly. Thanks. I really appreciate it."

"No problem. Just get it here before five."

I wrote down the address and got off the phone. It was already three-thirty. I had to work fast. Brenda called the messenger service to schedule a pick up while I took care of the disc. We had it out the door in thirty minutes, not bad for someone who's always behind the digital learning curve.

After that, I sat back in the chair and thought about my next move. I wanted to head Southside, but I didn't want to roll into the bar at six and sit there for three hours waiting for Conrad to show up. That wouldn't look suspicious at all. I told Dr. Halgrave I work cases from multiple angles which was true. So far, I'd been focused only on the security footage. A blurry image may or may not lead anywhere, so it was time to look elsewhere.

I punched the intercom button on the desk phone. "Hey Brenda, I got a job for you."

The internet makes my job both easier and more difficult at the same time. There's a lot of information available, which is good, but there's so much and from sketchy sources, it can be difficult to verify. I asked Brenda to start researching the black market for middle-eastern artifacts. This was an area I knew nothing about, and any background information would be helpful.

While Brenda worked on that, I went to the library to do some research on my own. I could have called Dr. Halgrave. She was the expert on this artifact, after all. And while it may come to that, I wanted to look into it on my own first.

Walking into the main branch of the Chicago Public Library can feel a little daunting with nine floors of books to choose from, but I had an idea of where to start. I took the elevator to the sixth floor which housed the Social Science and History section. A quick search through the online card catalog narrowed my destination even further.

Halgrave told me the missing artifact was presumed to be a representation of the ancient god Baal. I knew nothing of ancient religions, so that was where I began. Two hours later, a pile of books sat on the study table I'd claimed, and my head swam with all the new information. Navigating the ancient religions of the Middle East was like trying to cross a mosh pit at a Slayer concert. There were so many factions competing for dominance, it was hard to keep track. My brain was starting to hurt just thinking about it. It wasn't one of the debilitating headaches from earlier, but frustrating just the same.

I left the books where they lay and decided it was time to play darts.

***

The bartender at Smitty's recognized me as soon as I walked through the door. Guess that tip I left yesterday did the job. I took off my gloves and stuffed them in a pocket then stripped off the coat, glancing around for somewhere to hang it. The bartender motioned to a strip of hooks screwed to the wall to the right of the door. I hung it up and looked to see if Conrad was here. I didn't see him, but I did take note of two other patrons reclined at a table draining a pitcher of beer and three more that sat at the bar nursing their own pints.

I sidled up to the bar as well and said, "What's good tonight?"

"Burger's always good," the bald man answered as he reached into the sliding door of a cooler and withdrew a longneck.

"What about hot wings?"

"Oh yeah. You want regular hot, Mexican hot, or shit fire for a week hot?"

"Regular hot, I guess." I generally like spicy foods, but I also didn't want to go overboard without knowing what I was getting into.

"Drink?"

"Gin and tonic."

He nodded, then punched my order into the computer behind him before making my cocktail.

"How's the case going?" he asked.

I shrugged. Since I'd told him I was working in the neighborhood and that I was a PI, it was a logical question to ask. I decided to be honest, but vague, and talk about the museum case.

"Not great. Having a hard time turning up any useful info." I stretched my shoulders, rolled my neck, and took another look around the bar. At the back was a tiny hallway that probably led to the kitchen. I didn't see any restrooms, so I asked about them and was told they were down there too.

I took another sip, then slipped off the stool and crossed to the hallway. A dartboard hung on the back wall, and the space in front of it was kept clear of tables and chairs. No darts though. They must be behind the bar.

After a quick trip to the bathroom, which I discovered did not have a window leading to a back alley somewhere, I returned to my spot at the bar to await the arrival of my dinner.

The wings turned out to be okay. Not great, but not bad either. When I finished eating, I ordered another gin then slipped my coat back on and went outside for a smoke. It was getting colder, and it smelled like snow.

Over the last week, strings of lights had appeared running along roofs and framing windows with a seasonal glow. Standing here in the dark, looking out at them, I felt the sting of Christmas past that usually snuck up on me about this time of year.

It had been a long time since I'd had a Christmas proper. When I was a kid, Christmas was magical. The lights, and trees, and carols, and Santa, and presents enthralled me the whole month of December. There was always eggnog and cider, fruit cake and sugar cookies. And of course, Ralphie and Randy. What a classic.

After my mother passed away, Dad and I tried to hang on to some traditions, but it wasn't the same. Then, when he'd kicked the bucket, Christmas had become just a day off. With no family, it's hard to keep the magic alive.

Then I thought about Maggie and Alice. It would be their first Christmas without Frank. I felt a shadow, that had nothing to do with the passing headlights, creeping up on me. I flicked the rest of the cigarette into the street and went back inside.

I grabbed my drink off the bar and sucked it down to ward off the chill fingers worming their way into my guts, then asked about darts. Baldy passed over two sets and told me to return them when I was done. I ordered another gin. I'd have to make it last. Getting drunk was the last thing I wanted to do tonight.

One of the guys sitting at the bar glanced up at me, and I caught his eye.

"Wanna play?" I asked.

He shrugged, but stood up, drink in hand. We walked to the back and settled our drinks on the closest table.

"I'm Gray," I said, proffering my hand.

The guy shook it and replied, "Shane." That was it.

I took a couple of practice throws and landed them all over the board. I hadn't played darts in ages. Shane went next and got two of them in the red.

"Don't think I'll be putting any money on this game," I said.

He chuckled.

We each took a few more warm-up throws before officially starting a game. He beat me handily, but my aim was improving. I returned to my drink before starting another game.

"I take it you play on a regular basis?" I asked.

"Yep. Standing game every Thursday." He looked toward the front of the bar. "Alex should be here shortly."

"Oh. Will it be a problem if I play, too?"

"Depends. Loser buys the next round. That a problem?"

I looked thoughtful for a moment. "Is Alex any good?"

"Not as good as me," he said with a smile.

"Okay, then. Guess I need to dial in."

We were halfway through another game when Conrad showed up. He strolled through the door, hung up his coat, and ordered a beer before heading our way. He looked me up and down, then turned to Shane. "Who's the new guy?"

Shane shrugged again. "Calls himself Gray. Not very good, but he agreed to the terms."

Conrad regarded me again, eyes narrowing. "Could be hustling us."

"Could be," I agreed. "Only one way to find out."

Conrad laughed and pulled a small square box out of his back pocket. It was made of a dark, polished wood. "Only one way to find out," he agreed. He opened the box and withdrew three very professional looking darts.

I shot a dark look at Shane who shrugged yet again. "Great," I muttered.

With introductions out of the way, the game began. It was over quickly, and I lost horribly. True to my word, I bought their next round. Fortunately, they were cheap dates, preferring a domestic lager to anything else. They lightened up after that, chatting easily and asking about me. I told them I was a PI and a former cop, which piqued Conrad's interest and we talked about the department and which districts we worked.

The conversation was going exactly the way I'd hoped.

I lost the second game, too. Though not as badly.

As we waited for Shane to return with another two beers, both going on my tab, Conrad spoke up. "Gray. Your name sounds familiar, but I don't recognize you."

"I kind of made a splash in the papers a couple months ago. My name was kept out of it, but I'm sure it was in the official paperwork." I was still sipping on my second gin, trying to gauge his reaction. "You might have read about me."

He thought for a moment then said, "Wait, the Navy Pier thing? That was you?"

"Guilty."

He let out a low whistle. "Damn. That was some serious shit."

"You're telling me." Now it was time to cast bait. "And to think the whole thing was over a missing girl."

"Missing girl? I thought they'd kidnapped your partner."

"Oh, they did. But they did that because I discovered their trafficking ring while looking for a missing girl."

"Really?"

"That's what I figure." Now it was time to see if he took the bait. If he was a decent detective at all, he wouldn't be able to resist.

"Who was the girl?" Bingo.

"Nobody special. Her name's Ellie McCarthy."

"McCarthy? Hang on a second. That was my case."

"You're kidding." I tried to sound surprised. If he thought I was ambushing him, he'd get defensive and clam up.

"No. Damn. I hated putting that one aside. I'm glad you found her." Put it aside? What did that mean?

"What do you mean you hated putting it aside?" I asked.

"The lieutenant assigned me other cases with higher priority. I didn't even have a chance to get into it. All I'd done was interview her father. Running it down would have taken a lot of time, but the lieutenant said that time was better spent elsewhere, so I never got around to it. You know how it is."

I did know how it was. A lot of crimes happened in the city. A lot of reports are filed, but there simply aren't enough people to work the cases. A single detective might have a dozen or more on his caseload. Some took priority. Others were left on the back burner.

"Well, glad to hear it had nothing to do with poor detective work," I said.

He stiffened and narrowed his eyes. Most of us detectives have a pretty big ego and don't like having our skills insulted. I gazed back, wondering how he would react. I was joking, of course, and hoped he could tell. After a moment, he relaxed and said, "Yeah. Galls me, though, that some PI gets the credit for solving it."

I laughed. It was the perfect retort. My gut told me that Conrad was a decent guy, that he was just following orders and didn't question them. If it had been me, I probably would have kept nosing around, but that's me. I never followed orders that well. Some guys, though, did what they were told and kept their noses clean. They're the ones that retired with a nice pension and several medals to display on the mantle instead of having to find a new career before they hit forty.

At least now, I had a new direction to look. Wiggins was the lieutenant Conrad spoke of. It was time to dig into his dirty laundry. I wanted to keep the conversation going, but my phone rang. The number wasn't familiar, so I answered.

"Hello, Mr. Gray. This is Dr. Iasis. I was wondering if I could take you up on that cup of coffee."

9

The old man ran his knobby, skeletal fingers over the rough stone of the idol. Doing so almost felt like sacrilege because he delighted in it. Delight in such an abomination was blasphemy. The delight, however, came not from the simple possession of the item, but in the accomplishment of having acquired it. His order had sought this artifact for centuries, the legend passed down generation after generation. Now, finally, it was his.

This was only a piece of the puzzle, however. Though the legends spoke of its power, they did not provide instructions on how to access it. That part still remained a mystery. Until it could be discovered, the key found, it was nothing more than an ancient lump of sandstone.

But they would figure it out. Of that, he was certain. It was only a matter of time. And when they did, things would change. The paradigm would shift, and he would achieve what none before him had. Victory over the Infidel.

The other man in the room spoke. "What's so important about that thing?" He had taken a big risk to retrieve it. He felt he deserved some answers.

"It is an integral part of our plan," rasped the old man. "You have done well. You're certain you were not discovered?"

"As sure as I can be. Trust me, I've got a lot more

riding on this than you do." The thief peered at the old man. The cowl of his dark rose-colored robes hid his face as they always did. Though they had a common enemy, the secrecy surrounding this man was unsettling. "What does it do?" he asked, gesturing to the statue.

"It is hard to say. There are rumors, legends, but its exact nature is still unknown."

The thief's face fell. He had gone to a lot of trouble and for what? Why did they want it so bad if they didn't know what it did?

The old man must have sensed his disappointment because he said, "But at the heart of all legends lies the truth. And they all speak of the power to control its creator. While we may not possess all of its secrets yet, rest assured that all will be revealed."

The power to control its creator. That would be something.

"So what should I do now?"

"Go home. Go back to work. Forget about the idol. If we have need of you in the future, we will be in touch."

That's not what he wanted to hear. Now that he was involved, he felt there should be something...more—a bigger role to play in what was coming, perhaps. But do nothing? He sighed. What else could he do? He had waited a long time for this opportunity. He could wait a lot longer, he supposed. Without another word, he turned and left.

The old man watched him go, then returned his

gaze to the idol. Unlocking its secrets would demand his full attention. He stood with a creak and shuffled down the dimly lit hall to his room, closed the door behind him, and placed the statue on the small wooden desk.

He would spend this night praying for answers.

10

Clarke's Diner is somewhat of a landmark in Chicago. Although it closed down for a while, it reopened its doors and was met with joyous acclaim. Situated on Belmont just east of the train, it's a popular spot at all hours—mainly because it's open any time, day or night. It's also a hell of a lot better than the Deluxe Diner in my neighborhood.

Skipping out on the dart game was easy when I told them I had an impromptu date. Besides, I had all the information I needed for the moment, so I hauled ass to Lakeview.

Parking is the biggest problem in that area. If it isn't permit only on the side streets, spots get snapped up as soon as they're available. I had to drive around far too long before finding one four blocks away. From there I made a mad dash to the diner. The good doctor and I had agreed to meet at ten o'clock. It was already a quarter after. I had texted her when I got to the neighborhood but being this late wouldn't leave a very good impression.

Fortunately, she was waiting patiently when I arrived, panting to catch my breath. She sat alone in the corner booth by a window. As soon as I caught sight of her, my heart skipped a beat. It was nothing like the intense desire that had overcome me when I'd seen Dr. Halgrave the first time. This seemed more natural, like the butterflies of a high school crush.

She looked up and smiled as I slid into the booth across from her.

"Hi," I said. "Fancy meeting you here." Boy, was I good with opening lines. I must have blushed at my own awkwardness because her smile deepened.

"I'm glad you came," she said. "I wanted to apologize for my...rude behavior the other night."

"No need," I told her. "It was understandable. Who talks to some schmuck they meet in a dark alley in the middle of the night?"

"Still, I'm sorry. This is a little late, but I'm Stacy." She offered me her hand.

I took it gently and replied, "Gray. It's a pleasure to officially meet you."

The waitress came by and took our drink orders. We both got coffee. Black.

"Speaking of the other night, I should thank you again. You certainly handled that chef better than I could have."

"We have a history," she admitted.

"How so?"

"The Greek community is a pretty small one. I treat a lot of people who can't afford insurance or the price of an actual doctor visit."

"Aren't you an actual doctor?"

"Yes, but I make house calls, or work calls, as was

the case the other night. I've helped Markos's mother on more than one occasion. He's a tough guy, but I know how to push his buttons. How, exactly, did you find yourself staring down that cleaver of his?" she asked.

"I was working a job. His boss was skimming from the owner, and Markos was helping. They made me and didn't want the cat let out of the bag, I guess."

She shook her head slowly and sighed. "It would be something like that. He always did have more bluster than brains."

"Sorry," I said, not sure what else to say. The waitress came by and dropped off our coffees. We sat there in silence for a moment as we sipped. Before it got awkward, I spoke again. "So how come you changed your mind? About the coffee, I mean?"

She didn't answer right away. She seemed to be considering her answer carefully.

"Honestly, I had kind of forgotten about you." Well, that stung. "It had been a really long day when we met outside Moxy and the whole night was just kind of a blur. But when you came to the ER this morning with your niece, I remembered." I thought about correcting her but didn't. My relationship with Maggie wasn't really at issue. "Of course, there was more to it than that. When your niece started talking about how quickly your jaw had healed, it rang a bell. It seems there's been some talk about you around the hospital. I admit that it piqued my interest."

This wasn't what I had expected. She only wanted to meet because of a medical anomaly? I was starting to think this wasn't much of a date at all. I had to salvage this.

"I see," I said. "So, it had nothing to do with my rugged good looks?" I flashed a goofy grin. The corner of her mouth quirked up in a half smile. Huh. That should have been good for a chuckle at least.

"Maybe," she admitted. "You are handsome, but considering the extent of your injuries, you probably shouldn't be."

Was that a compliment? I couldn't read this woman at all. Reading people had never been a problem for me. My problem had always been not screwing things up.

"You sure know how to flatter a fella, don't you?"

Her cheeks flushed at that. "I'm sorry. I'm not doing a very good job at this. I usually have better bedside manner." She shifted in her seat and took a long drink of coffee before continuing. "The truth is, I liked how you talked to your niece. I overheard your conversation before I came in. You didn't talk down to her and you didn't tell her what to do. It was refreshing. After you left, I did some digging. I pulled your file and looked at your records."

"You pulled my file?" I interrupted. "Isn't that against the rules if I'm not your patient?" She stared at her coffee even more chagrined. "Not that I wouldn't have done the same thing myself, but I have a reputation for coloring outside the lines."

She looked up. "It was not the most ethical of actions. But I had to see for myself."

"See what?"

"If the rumors were true." This was heading into uncomfortable territory. I didn't want to lie to Stacy, but she'd think I was nuts if I told her what really happened. It was time for evasive action. Otherwise known as non-committal grunts and shrugs.

"And?"

"And, there is quite a bit of controversy surrounding your miraculous recovery. Despite what you told your niece, your jaw was severely broken. The x-rays show that clearly. You should have been drinking through a straw for weeks." Her tone simmered with excitement instead of the incredulity I'd expected.

"So, I've been told."

"But that's not all. Your zygomatic arch and nasal bone were also fractured. Yet here you are, right as rain."

"Uh..." I was stuck on the big z-word and didn't know how to respond. Luckily my plan was to play stupid anyway.

"Instances of accelerated healing like you've displayed are extremely rare," she continued. Her voice pitched higher. The words came quickly and she leaned forward. "I've only seen two cases and that's a lot. Most doctors go their entire careers without ever seeing anything like it, and of those that appear to display such healing, half are actually a misdiagnosis to begin with."

I found myself being drawn in by her enthusiasm. "So, it does happen. Any idea why?"

"No, none. There isn't any research on the subject. Most incidents get labeled as a fluke, or the patients either fall off the radar or refuse to be examined further. The first time I saw it, I was working a late shift at the ER. A wagon brought in a John Doe with multiple gunshot wounds. I figured they'd pronounce quickly. He was a mess. But instead, he survived the surgery. That, in and of itself, was pretty miraculous. But the next day, he woke up, pulled out the IVs, and walked out of the hospital."

I knew exactly the kind of thing she was talking about, but if I told her everything I'd seen, she'd have me committed. So, I just nodded.

"Ever since then, I've wanted to know more. If we could figure out why these very few people have the ability to heal faster, the impact on the medical world would be enormous."

"And you were hoping I'd consent to being your lab rat." It wasn't a difficult conclusion to make.

She deflated at my comment, the fire of her excitement quenched as she realized how her confession must have sounded. "Actually," she said in a more subdued, but no less earnest tone, "I wanted to pick your brain first. Hear your story. Many doctors aren't very good at listening, myself included. Here I am rambling on about what I want and haven't let you get a word in edgewise. I'm sorry."

"It's alright," I assured her. "It's kind of nice not to have to ask all the questions. Usually, I have to work a lot harder to get information out of people." I smiled and she smiled back. "Let me ask you a question, then."

I wasn't sure how much I'd be able to tell her, but vagaries shouldn't be hard to invent. I took a swallow of coffee and nodded at her over the brim.

"How long have you known about your ability?"

That was easy. "It's a rather recent...development. Did my records show any broken ribs?" She nodded. "Well, that happened only a couple days before the other thing." Her eyebrows rose at that. "That was the first time I had any clue."

She reached for her coffee again, and little lines appeared across her forehead as she thought about what to ask next. It was adorable. "What's it like?"

That seemed a rather broad question, so I asked for clarification.

"Did you know it was happening? Did you feel anything when it was?"

I considered my answer carefully before responding. "No, I didn't know what was happening at the time. It was only when the doctors were surprised by my recovery that I realized what had happened. Although, looking back, I suppose I knew that something was going on." I paused, thinking about those words. They weren't entirely accurate, and I felt the need to expand. "I don't want to give you the wrong idea. It's not like breathing, not something that happens automatically. Ugh, this is hard to explain." I looked at her, not realizing my eyes had been elsewhere. She was watching—and listening—intently. "I wasn't thinking straight after my injuries. The world was pretty messed up from my perspective. I think I went into some sort or trance or something that may have triggered this accelerated healing."

"If you cut yourself right now, it wouldn't heal up within a day?" she asked.

"I don't think so."

Her eyes unfocused as her thoughts drifted away, pondering the significance of what I'd said. After a minute, she refocused on me and gave a warm smile. There was something different about her gaze now. It was like a starving person had just been given a sandwich and could now focus on building a house, or making art, or something other than mere survival.

"Tell me about your family," she said.

We chatted for another hour about all sorts of things. She told me about her family, and I told her about losing Frank and my relationship with his. We talked about our favorite foods, our favorite places in the city. It was nice. It was like we were actually on a date, something I hadn't done in a very long time.

Finally, she looked at her watch and swore when she saw how late it was. Then she apologized for her language. It was all I could do not to giggle at how cute it was. Then I almost gagged at how ridiculous I was being. I'm a grown man for crying out loud. But still.

I offered to walk her to her car which was parked several blocks away and she graciously accepted.

It had gotten bitterly cold in the last hour, so we both bundled up and set a brisk pace down the sidewalk. We were heading north from Belmont and had gone two blocks when I heard the rustle of clothing behind. I shot a glance over my shoulder, not liking what I saw: nothing.

Someone was behind us, but they were keeping to the shadows. My brain went on full alert and I paid a whole lot more attention to our surroundings.

I leaned over and whispered to Stacy, "Don't freak out, but I think we're being followed."

She simply nodded and quickened her steps.

We didn't make it to her car.

Halfway down the block, our pursuer caught up. I spun around as I heard footfalls on the sidewalk and was met with the sight of someone pointing a gun at us. He was only a head shorter than me and was bundled up against the cold. He wore a dark ski mask that hid his identity and kept his face from freezing. I wished I had one. My lips were getting stiff.

"Don't move," he said. His voice was deep, and it cut through the frigid night air.

Stacy had also turned around and now hugged her handbag close.

"I said don't move," the man repeated, pointing his gun with emphasis.

"What do you want?" I asked calmly.

"Your wallet and her purse." He gestured to Stacy with the barrel where he left it pointing.

"Alright, I'm going to reach inside my coat and get it out. Don't shoot me."

When confronted with an armed mugger, the safest thing to do is comply and give them your valuables. Once they have what they want, they'll usually run off and leave you alone. This is especially true if they are armed with a gun. If the guy had a knife, I'd make a move for my piece, which was tucked neatly in the holster at my side. But he didn't, so that was a bad idea.

I carefully unbuttoned the top of my coat, but the guy pointed the gun back at me. "What are you doing?" My hand froze.

"I told you. I'm going to get my wallet out of my pocket. Is that okay?"

The mugger thought for a second, then said, "Yeah, okay."

As I worked the next button loose, Stacy held her bag out toward the man, who was too far away to reach it. As she did, the bag tumbled from her grasp. It landed on the sidewalk, its contents spilling out.

"I'm sorry," she blurted. "I'll pick it up."

The mugger swung the gun back on her. "No, you won't. I'll get it." He took a few steps closer, so he was within reach of the bag. He kept the gun trained on her. He looked down at the bag to see what had fallen out of it.

Stacy lunged forward, and her left hand shot out, slapping the pistol to the side. It was a risky move. He could have squeezed off a round, injuring her, me, or any number of innocent people nearby. Her right arm followed through, striking a vicious blow to the would-be thief's solar plexus, driving the air from his lungs and knocking him off-balance. He dropped the gun and it clattered to the ground. It happened fast, but I already had my hand inside my coat, gripping my own weapon.

Stacy continued her assault. She launched a kick hard between the guy's legs and the fight went out of him. He collapsed to the ground, writhing in pain.

By this point I had my .380 trained on him. Stacy bent down to pick up the mugger's gun, but I stopped her. "Don't touch it," I said simply. She nodded and knelt instead to pick up the contents of her bag. "That either."

I dialed 9-1-1 and we waited patiently for the cops

to arrive. It would have been so much easier if I still carried cuffs. Warmer too. By the time they got there, Stacy's teeth were chattering, and I was pretty sure my toes were turning blue. At least they let us sit in the patrol car while we gave our statements.

After that, we found Stacy's car and she kindly drove me to mine. I thought a lot about what she'd done. She'd taken a huge risk. Fortunately, it had paid off and no one had been hurt.

"That was impressive," I told her. "Risky, but impressive."

"I don't like being bullied." Her tone was assertive, but as I watched her, I saw regret in her eyes too.

"I guess not." I pointed out the Buick and she pulled up beside it. "Where did you learn that technique?"

She hesitated before answering. "You know how I got started in medicine?"

I shrugged. "Nope."

"I joined the army when I was eighteen and went the combat medic route. It was the only way I could afford the education. While I was there, I took an interest in the hand-to-hand stuff. I wasn't special forces, so they didn't really train me for it, but I stuck with it when I left. The city can be a dangerous place, especially for a single woman. I've been studying Vale Tudo for years. I guess you just saw my dark side."

"Dark side?"

"The other side of the coin?"

I stared at her.

She sighed. "I'm a doctor. I help people. I'm not supposed to hurt them."

"Who said you can't do both?"

A smile played across her lips. "I'm going to call you in a day or two," she said matter-of-factly as I climbed out.

I smiled, not trusting myself to speak. *Who was this woman?* I thought as she drove off down the street. Not only was she a doctor, but she was a bad-ass, too. I hoped this was the beginning of something beautiful.

11

"She's cute. Not my type, though." The old man sat in the booth next to me. I started and looked over. How the hell had he gotten there? Looking back at Stacy, who sat there looking intently at me with a small smile, I realized she must not be able to see him. An unsettling feeling grew in the pit of my stomach.

I glanced around the diner and saw indistinguishable faces at the various tables. I couldn't pick out any identifying features on anyone. And now that I was paying attention, I realized there were no discernible words in the surrounding conversation.

What was going on? Hadn't I already left the diner anyway?

I turned back to the old man. "I'm dreaming again, aren't I?"

"Of course, boy," he said. He picked a cup of coffee off the table that hadn't been there before and took a swig. He made a thoughtful face and took another. "Only way I can talk to you."

I looked around the diner again and shook my head. "Thought I would have picked up on more detail."

"Guess you were distracted," he said.

I looked back to Stacy who still stared straight ahead. It was getting creepy. "Can we go somewhere else?"

He shrugged and the diner vanished. Now we sat on a concrete step beside Lake Michigan. Lights twinkled in the darkness on the water's surface. This was one of the places I went when I wanted to be around nature. It was peaceful.

"You still live," the grizzled old man commented. "You fixed the problem?"

I nodded. "So, it would seem."

"Good."

"What should I call you?" I asked. Our last meeting had been strained and he'd left me a with a zillion questions. Now, however, he seemed more relaxed.

"I've gone by many names over the years, but I don't think any of them are fitting for this time and place. Call me what you will."

I continued to stare out over the lake. There was something familiar about the old man. A feeling that I already knew him had been building since our last encounter. The thought was outlandish, but the fact that he was here, that any of this was actually happening, was completely ridiculous to begin with. So, I went with it.

"Willy, I think I'll call you Willy."

A tiny smile tugged at his lips and he nodded once.

Thoughts swirled around my brain like leaves caught in a dust-devil. I had so many questions, but my gut said I didn't have time to ask very many. Which one to ask first? Did I go for background information, an explanation on what was happening to me? He seemed to know something about it.

Maybe I should find out more about him. What was he exactly? How did he know what was happening? Why should I trust him? The answer to that seemed pretty clear. He had saved my life. What should I do about that? I didn't like being in anyone's debt.

I watched the leaf-questions whip around, eyeing each one. Finally, I plucked one from the torrent, deciding it was the best choice. "What should I do now?"

Old-man Willy raised his one bushy eyebrow. "Interesting choice." He said it like he, too, had watched the questions swirling around. Hell, maybe he had. "What makes you think I know?"

I gave a him a sidelong glance. "You saved my life. Twice. You inserted yourself into my dreams to warn me. You explained the danger in a logical way that I could understand. Seems you know a hell of a lot more about what's going on than I do. I also don't figure you for the kind of guy to just pop in without a reason. Which means there's something else you want to tell me."

He nodded. "You should learn more about what you can do."

"Okay," I said. "You volunteering to teach me?"

"I'm afraid I can't," he replied with a shrug. "As I said before, I don't know how you can do the things you do. I only know that you can."

"How do you know what I *can* do, then?"

"Must a child be able to explain *how* a bird can fly to know that it soars through the air?"

Simple observation, then. Which meant he had seen someone like me before. "So, there are others like me?"

"No. Not anymore." That didn't sound good, but I didn't say anything. He continued. "I have known others with your gift. It was long ago, but I have a very long memory. You already know about the added strength and accelerated healing. Tracking is another."

"Tracking? You mean finding people? I already do that."

"Yes, but can you tell me exactly how many people are in your building at any given time? Can you follow a trail with no trace of physical evidence?"

I didn't answer.

***

The next morning, I rolled out of bed, showered, dressed, and walked down the street to a convenience store. I bought three cans of tuna and one of evaporated milk. I took these back to the apartment. I dumped one can of tuna into a glass bowl, punched a hole in the can of milk and poured a third of it into another dish and set both of them on the kitchen floor. Then I remembered there was no litter box. I stared hard at the orange tabby draped across the back of my sofa. He stared lazily back.

"Okay, I'm leaving the lid up and the seat down," I told him. "Don't shit on the floor."

Half an hour later, I was riding the Red Line south. I spent most of my life in the city without a vehicle, except when I was in a police cruiser, but that was a while ago. There's a sense of freedom that accompanies public transportation. It isn't the same kind of freedom that comes with your own car, one of convenience, but a more cerebral freedom. Driving requires every brain cell to be focused on the task at hand; there's no room for error without risking a major accident. When you're on a bus or train speeding toward your destination, however, your mind is free to focus on anything at all. Since the Deluxe Diner was busy during breakfast, the train was the next best place for me to think.

It was early, and the morning rush was in progress, but this far north, finding a seat wasn't a problem. It would be standing room only by the time we hit the Belmont stop. In other places, that many people would mean distractions out the wazoo. But there's an unspoken code of conduct among commuters on the train. No eye contact. No conversation. No disruption to the routine. It was like being in the eye of a hurricane. Plenty of activity all around, but safe in your own little bubble of solitude.

I slid my bulk into an empty window seat halfway down the car. A woman sat directly in front of me, a head full of dark hair. Across the aisle two young men sat next to each other. Roommates probably. One bobbed his head to music pumped through a set of noise-canceling head-phones. The other read a book.

I settled my weight into the seat, letting the mold-ed plastic support me. I relaxed into it and closed my eyes. Conjuring a mental picture of the red and blue lights from my dreams, the source of strength and heal-ing, I concentrated hard and focused intently until the im-age was cemented firmly in my brain. I took a deep breath then opened my eyes.

Dark hair swayed straight ahead as the train rocked on the tracks. A head bobbed across the aisle, and a man turned a page in his book. There were no blue lights other than the sparking of the electrified rail out-side.

I closed my eyes again. This time I concentrated even harder, putting all my thought and focus into a sin-gle image. Again, I opened my eyes. And saw nothing new. No wisp of energy. No writhing, undulating cords. Why wasn't it working?

The other times I had seen the lights, I had been asleep, dreaming. Or maybe it wasn't dreaming, exactly. Some form of astral projection or something.

I'd only seen them once while awake. And I defi-nitely wasn't concentrating on them then. I'd been too busy trying not to die.

Maybe I was concentrating too hard. Maybe I needed to go to the other side of the spectrum. Maybe it was about relaxation.

A few years back I'd gone to a trade show that had lots of new-fangled technological gadgets. Spy gear, mostly. Tiny HD cameras that broadcast signals wirelessly, the latest GPS trackers to sync with a smartphone, drones, that sort of thing. One booth displayed the latest in brainwave-controlled software. There was a headset supporting little electrodes that measured brain activity which, in turn, was used to control little people on a computer screen. It looked cool, so I tried it out. I discovered pretty quickly that the character responded best when I emptied my mind and focused on nothing rather than concentrating on what I wanted it to do.

Maybe that's how this worked. Like one of those magic eye pictures from the nineties that you could only see if you let your eyes go unfocused. So, that's what I did. Instead of concentrating, I let my mind go out of focus, not holding on to any one thought, completely relaxed. A Zen state of mind.

As my consciousness drifted, almost detaching from my physical body, the world dimmed, like watching a movie slip from ultra HD to old, grainy VHS home movies. Then the lights sprang into existence, ebbing and flowing aimlessly in all directions—a thousand, thousand threads of blue-white light seeping out of the dark-haired lady in front, the two guys on my left, every visible person on the train. There were threads of red interwoven among them. As they spilled down into the center of the car, they began to flow together, concentrating into slightly larger streams that dribbled through the shell of the train and out into the world beyond.

Instead of focusing on the lights, I watched them with the periphery of my awareness, like watching something in the edge of your vision. Doing this, I realized the lights weren't all the same color. Looking directly at them, they appeared either blue or red. But in the periphery, they took on more nuanced variations. The threads coming from the woman were whiter, the ones from headphone guy were tinted orange. Book guy was a deep navy.

We pulled into the Lawrence stop, and a small wave of people boarded. The streams of energy were suddenly joined by a cascade of new threads. The process repeated itself at every stop until people were jammed into the train with standing room only, the energy no longer a meandering stream but a rushing torrent swirling around hundreds of legs.

I focused my mind back on the immediate surroundings. The crush of people, the curving lines of the hard plastic seats snapped into crystal clarity, and the lights vanished.

We continued south and I practiced slipping in

and out of the trance-like state over and over until it became comfortable. As we approached the loop, passengers disembarked. They left little pools of light behind and lingering trails that shimmered in their wake. This phenomenon intrigued me, considering what Willy had said. Perhaps these trails were unique to the person that created them and could be followed like a bloodhound does with scent.

I chose a person hanging tight to one of the handrails. My only criteria was that he was nondescript. Just your average Joe heading to work, dressed similarly to everyone else. I studied the energy seeping from him, judging its color. It was blue with a hint of gray—similar to many others, but not exact. I kept my awareness tuned to it until we hit downtown.

The guy got off the train at Monroe. I stayed on until the next stop. The Redline was underground here, the platform a wide concrete strip between the north and southbound tracks. There were no barriers between stops. One could easily walk from Lake Street all the way south to Van Buren, a total of seven full city blocks, without ever stepping foot off the platform.

Stepping off the train, I turned north and went back to the Monroe stop. I stood still and let the world go fuzzy until the lights appeared. I stood there for a long moment, maybe two, awed by the torrent of lights surging through the tunnel. The streams from the trains, converged with a river of energy coursing beneath the streets, mind-blowing in its magnitude—maybe literally if not for my psychic lightning rod or whatever.

Finally recovering, I ambled over to one of the exits. The flow lessened somewhat, but it was still impossible to discern a single individual's contribution.

I stepped on the escalator and rode it up into the morning light. On the surface, the flow of energy was more spread out, wide but shallow, and I could pick out strands that led into surrounding buildings.

I looked for my anonymous quarry's trail for a good ten minutes before giving up. There was simply too much going on here to single him out. Maybe in a less populous area it would be easier. Frustrated, I decided to come back to this problem. I had other things to do. I needed to check in with Brenda and find out what she'd learned about the antique black market.

As I reached for the phone, it buzzed in my pocket.

12

It wasn't a phone call. It was an email. From Eddie Vallard.

There was no text, just an attached image. Apparently, his software had finished doing whatever it did, and this was the result. The phone's screen was too small for me to see it clearly, so I crossed over a couple of blocks and hopped on the Brown Line back to the office.

By the time I got there, it was late morning and lunchtime was fast approaching. I stuck my head into Brenda's office. "Lunch?"

"Packed," she said. "Dr. Halgrave called from the museum. She wants an update."

"Of course," I said. I didn't have any new information yet, but I might soon, so I didn't plan on making the call until then.

I booted up the old PC. The tower whirred and buzzed as it came to life. It would take a few minutes, so I hit the kitchen to make a fresh pot of coffee. While the coffee perked, I stepped outside for a smoke. By the time the cigarette and coffee were done, the computer was all ready to go. Even though my computer was slow, our internet was fast, and I had Eddie's email open and was staring at a photo of the mystery man from the museum within seconds. It filled the entire screen. No problem seeing it now. I studied it carefully, hoping to glean some new information. He was average height, average build. There was no bare skin visible. He could have been black, white, or purple for all I could tell. But he wasn't blonde. Dark hair poked out around the back of the ball cap. The most distinguishing feature I could see was the logo on his jacket.

Tracking down the company or brand that belongs to a logo is harder than you'd think. Most people think of the golden arches or the Nike swoosh when they think of logos. Sure, those are recognizable. But every small business and start-up trying to make a name for themselves hires a graphic artist to design one for fifty bucks. Logos are everywhere. They're supposed to be memorable, but unless you spend a fortune putting it out into the world with advertising, nobody will remember it. Google's image search can make it easier, but only if there's a significant web presence.

Fortunately, I didn't need to worry about any of that. This particular logo had the name of the business right there, plain as day. Lon's Auto. A quick search told me it was a repair shop out in Albany Park. Bingo. Now we were getting somewhere.

I called the museum and asked to speak with Cleve. I was put on hold for several minutes while they tracked him down.

"Yeah," he said once he got to the phone. He sounded a little out of breath.

"Morning, Cleve. It's Detective Gray. I have one more question for you."

"Okay. Shoot."

"Know anybody that works at Lon's Auto?"

"Nope. Sorry."

"Fair enough. I need to speak with Dr. Halgrave, if you don't mind."

"Yeah, okay." There was a clatter and two beeps as Cleve fumbled with the phone. Then the line clicked and went to dial tone. I guess Cleve wasn't used to the phones.

I called back and got transferred again. Dr. Halgrave picked up on the third ring. "Hello?" she said.

"Hello," I said back. "This is Detective Gray."

"Mason," she said, her tone of voice turning syrupy sweet. "I'm so glad you called. I hope you have an update. Our donor is very...anxious...to have his piece returned." The slight pause before she said "anxious" made it clear a different word would better describe the reality of the situation. He'd probably chewed her out quite vehemently over the phone at least once already.

"I have something. I'm not sure where it will lead, but it's better than nothing."

She didn't say anything, but I could hear her lean into the phone, so I continued. "There was a newly installed camera, one that was overlooked in the initial footage that was sent. There's a person on it that no one can account for. There's no face, just a logo. Does Lon's Auto mean anything to you?"

"No," she said slowly. "No, I can't say it does."

"I'm going to head over there this afternoon. Sniff around a little. See if anything shakes loose. I'll let you know if I find anything."

"Excellent," she replied. She proceeded to give me her cell number. It was a 312 area code, a downtown prefix. Fancy. She asked me to call her on that number in the future. It was direct and I wouldn't have to go through the switchboard.

***

Albany Park is at the terminal end of the Brown Line. I grabbed a hot dog on the way to the train. Chili, mustard, and onion: the way a hot dog is supposed to taste. I spent most of the train ride practicing my waking trance. There weren't many people commuting out here this time of day, so I stared out the window, watching the city glide by, watching the network of lights spiderweb its way across the frozen ground, a blue and red glow against the dirty white of recent snow.

At the Kimball station, I eased off the train and carefully picked my way down the stairs and out onto the street. Maintaining the sight was easy sitting on the train. Walking around without bumping into things proved a bit more difficult. It could be done, but movement was slow and languorous because too much focus on the world would cause the vision to snap out of existence.

The river of lights was smaller here than downtown, perhaps due to fewer people being here, but it was still substantial. After a few minutes, I decided that it might be possible to follow the trail of energy left by a single person out here. There was no reason to do so at the moment, however, so I let the thought go as well as the sight, and walked west on Lawrence.

It was a wide avenue with two and three story buildings packed tight on either side; their storefronts on the bottom and apartments above. Currency exchanges, cell phone shops, and convenience stores all huddled together. Green awnings with white lettering advertised anything a person heading home from the train could possibly need. Four blocks later, I crossed at a light and walked north on a side street. Lon's Auto was situated a block and a half away from the main drag.

It was a decent-sized repair shop built into a square brick building. A white metal sign with the now familiar logo hung bolted to the outside wall just above a glass door sporting several automotive decals. The whine of pneumatic tools and wispy clouds of steam and exhaust wafted out of two roll-up garage doors gaping open despite the freezing temperatures. A small fenced lot across the street held several vehicles either waiting to be serviced or to be picked up by their owners.

I stepped through one of the garage doors. The

temperature rose several degrees, but not enough to be warm. It was louder inside. Two guys were pulling wheels off of a blue Ford Escort held aloft by a hydraulic lift. I studied them, noting their distinguishing features, looking for anything that would eliminate them as suspects. Both were average height and build, one white and one black. One was bald, the other had dark hair. Another guy was ducked under the hood of a red Kia. He was smaller than the other two, but I couldn't see enough of him to tell anything else. Three men, who presumably all owned jackets with the shop logo printed on them. All three could be the guy I was looking for.

I stood patiently, waiting for someone to see me. One of the wheel men did take notice after a minute. He nodded an acknowledgment and came over once he'd dealt with the load in his arms.

"Hey buddy," he said. "What can I do for you?" He wore a pair of insulated coveralls. A white patch with red lettering sewed on the chest told me his name was Marcus.

"I'm looking for Lon," I told him.

"He's in the office." He pointed to another glass door in the side wall. I figured it connected to the waiting area where paperwork was kept, and payments were processed. I thanked him and went through. On the other side, four faded paisley chairs were lined up along the outside wall, scuffed and worn with age. Across from them sat an old metal desk littered with smudged calendars, receipts, and other unidentifiable papers. Behind it, a round man with a weathered face slouched in a cheap rolling office chair. His skin was dark, maybe from years of sun, maybe from years of grease and oil stains. He looked up as I stepped through the door.

"You Lon?" I asked.

He nodded and said, "What can I do for you?"

I reached into my coat pocket and took out a folded piece of paper with a picture of the man from the video footage. I had printed a copy before leaving the office. I unfolded it and held it out to him.

"That's your logo, right?"

He squinted and peered closely at the picture. "Looks like it."

"This was taken at the scene of a crime four days ago. This guy could be a key witness. Can you tell who it is?"

"You a cop or something?" he asked.

"Something," I said and showed him my credentials.

"Private Dick, huh? Like in one of them old movies? You working for some dame?" He grinned up at me.

"Actually, yes. Now look at the picture. Do you know who it is?"

Lon looked long and hard at the photo then finally

screwed up his face and shrugged. "Sorry pal. I can't tell you who it is. It's definitely one of our jackets though."

"Okay," I said. "Definitely one of your jackets. That's good. How many people have one?"

"Everybody that works here."

"I saw three guys in the back. Are there more?"

"Three others."

"Okay. Six guys. That narrows it down."

"Plus all the guys that used to work here but don't anymore," he added.

"How many is that?" I asked.

"I dunno. A dozen or so."

"That's still not terrible. You got contact info for them?"

He shook his head. "A few of them, maybe. But if they left more than five years ago, probably not."

"Okay," I said. "Let's start with the guys working today. Were they here on Monday?"

Lon swiveled around in his chair and pulled a clipboard off the wall. After perusing it a moment, he said, "Nah, Park and Heifers were off Monday."

"Can I talk to them?"

He squinted up at me. "You got a warrant?"

"No. I'm not a cop, remember. I'm not here to arrest anyone. I just need to ask some questions."

"Right." He shrugged. "They're in the garage. Just don't get in the way."

I nodded and pushed back through the glass door to the bays beyond. Lon came through a few seconds later, puffing like he'd just climbed a flight of stairs.

"Park! Heifers! Come here!" he bellowed over the din. The white guy looked over and the smaller one with his head buried in the Kia extracted himself from the engine compartment. Both crossed the floor to stand in front of us.

Lon jerked his head at me and said, "This guy wants to talk to you." Then he turned around and went back into the office.

The two guys looked at me but didn't say anything. The white guy's name tag read Matt. The other guy was Asian. Korean, probably, going by his name tag, which read Jin.

I pictured each of them wearing a jacket and baseball cap pulled low, back turned toward a video camera. Jin was smaller than Matt, but he wasn't a tiny guy. Either one of them could be my mystery guest at the museum. Marcus was in the clear. He'd been working the day of the theft.

I looked at the two guys in front of me and thought about my approach.

"I'm looking for a kid," I told them. "Her mom is worried sick. The cops got nothing so I'm trying to track down witnesses. A neighbor lady said she remembers somebody wearing a jacket around with the garage logo on it the morning the girl disappeared. I know it's a long shot, but maybe it was one of you two. Maybe you saw something that'll help us find her. Could you tell me where you were Monday morning?"

The guys looked at each other, deciding who would speak first. Jin finally opened his mouth. "I was probably sleeping. Monday is our day off. I don't normally get up until eleven or twelve those days." He spoke perfect English, though his accent was heavy.

I looked to Matt who was watching Jin and nodding. It took him a moment to realize I was waiting for him to say something.

"Oh, uh, Monday? What time?" he asked.

"Around ten o'clock," I said. "That's when she was last seen."

"Uh, ten o'clock...oh yeah, I was cruising back up Lakeshore on my bike."

"Lakeshore Drive? At ten in the morning? In December?"

He grinned. "Yeah. Traffic ain't bad by then and it's really invigorating."

"Right," I said, wondering at the word 'invigorating'. I'm sure it was true, but who says that? "Okay, I guess neither of you saw the girl then. Who else works here that might have been out and about on Monday morning?"

They looked at each other again. Jin shrugged and

said, "I dunno, man."

Matt said, "What about Ronnie?"

Jin nodded. "Maybe."

"Ask Lon. He can tell you," Matt said. Then both of them shuffled their feet like they wanted to get back to work, so I thanked them for their time and walked back into the office to get Ronnie's address.

13

I walked the seven blocks to the address Lon had given me. It was a basement apartment in a three-story converted single family house. The siding was a muted yellow with patches of green where moss and algae had settled in over years of neglect. Shutters hung in disrepair and a window on the third floor was boarded up. A cracked and crumbling sidewalk covered with a well-trod layer of snow and ice led through a chain-link fence and up to the front stoop. There was no gate, just an opening where a gate should be. If the outside looked this bad, the inside would be a dream.

A few cars were parked along the curb, but most spots were vacant, people having driven them to work hours ago. Across the street was a bright yellow 1995 Ford Mustang GTS. I'm not much of a car guy, but even I remembered it from high school. It was the must-have ride for cruising the avenue back in the day. This one had a rear spoiler and an intake on the hood. Clearly someone had done some work on it.

Also on the block, were an old green pickup with a ladder rack on the back and another Ford. This one a newer model, black with tinted windows and no hubcaps.

I turned back to the apartment and walked through the "gate." The apartment I was looking for was labeled C. Not 3, which would mean the third floor, but C, which was clearly the basement. Instead of climbing the stoop, I followed a branch of the sidewalk that went around the side of the building.

The sidewalk led to five concrete steps going down to a door at basement level. It was old, wooden, and solid on the bottom, with four small panes of glass near the top. There was only a single doorknob. No doorbell. No deadbolt.

I stepped down into the alcove and knocked on the door. There was no response. I knocked again. This time I called out, "Hey Ronnie, the guys at the shop sent me over." Still nothing.

I glanced over my shoulder at the black Ford parked on the street. Though I couldn't see anyone, I could feel someone watching me from behind the dark glass. My gut told me I needed to get in this apartment, though I had no idea what I would find. The door was certainly locked, so I didn't reach for the knob yet.

One good kick was all it would take to open it, but that would be too obvious. Picking it was the same story. I stood still, thinking, trying to look like I was waiting for someone to open up.

I let my eyes glaze over, shifting my awareness to that other place, and tendrils of light flared into existence. I studied them, watched their flow, deciding on the right one.

The red ones were dangerous. Yes, they made me

stronger, but they also made my blood boil with rage. While anger can be useful in certain situations, it's usually an impediment to rational thought. People don't think clearly when they're pissed off. They make poor choices that they regret later or, in a fight, mistakes that an opponent can exploit. On the other hand, anger can be used as fuel, a motivating force for justice. I didn't need all of that right now, but I did need a little boost of strength.

I chose a tiny thread of red light meandering just off to my right and plucked it between thumb and forefinger. Immediately, the thread responded, writhing and wriggling for a split second before sinking into my flesh and flowing up my arm. A burning, prickling sensation followed it and I felt a tiny flare of anger. *Not much, but enough*, I thought.

I grasped the doorknob in my right hand and gave it a quick twist. The locking mechanism inside caught, then popped as its inner workings were sheared in half. The knob turned freely then, and I jiggled it a little, causing the small piece of metal fitted into the frame to shift back inside the knob. The door swung open and I peered inside.

A bare bulb hung from the ceiling just inside and cast a pale-yellow circle of light on the foyer. I couldn't see much beyond the entryway. It was a basement apartment and what little light filtered through the half windows was further blocked by heavy curtains.

Instead of going inside, I turned and walked back up the steps, along the sidewalk and back to the street. I hung a left and walked the twenty yards to the black Ford and tapped my knuckles on the passenger side window.

After twenty seconds or so, it buzzed down.

Inside sat a man with a square jaw and five o'clock shadow in a rumpled brown suit. A Hardee's bag rested on the seat next to him and a giant coffee in the drink holder. Other than that, the car was spotless.

"Can I help you?" he asked.

"Maybe we can help each other, detective," I said. His eyes widened fractionally at that.

"How…" he began.

"Black Ford, tinted windows, no hubcaps, minimal salt and road grime. Not that hard to spot."

He sighed and his eyes narrowed. "Okay, how can we help each other?"

"I'm a private detective looking for the person that lives in the apartment you're watching. I'm betting you'd like nothing more than to get in there and take a look around, but you don't have a warrant, right?"

"Maybe," he said.

"Well, here's the thing. The door is unlocked and ajar. That seems rather suspicious to me. As a private citizen, I am concerned for the well-being of the resident. It could be that someone in there is hurt and needs help. I've just reported my concern and intent to an officer of the law. Pretty sure that constitutes probable cause."

He looked thoughtful while he processed this information then said, "What's in it for you?"

"I get back up."

After I showed him my credentials to prove I was who I said, he nodded, popped the door open, and slid out of the sedan. Together, we walked back to the fence, and I led the way to the basement door. I pointed out the broken doorknob and we had a brief staring contest over who would go first. There were no head nods, nothing spoken, not even a grunt—just a silent exchange of thought and intention. He made his point quickly, and I stepped back to let him through the door first.

Inside was a lazy excuse of a foyer, more like a closet, half illuminated by the naked bulb hanging above. The detective retrieved a small LED flashlight from a pocket and clicked it on. The beam was bright and steady, tinted blue. Not like the timid yellow beams of flashlights from a decade ago.

Ahead, a doorway opened into a larger room. The flashlight beam played over a small Formica-topped table and the hint of cabinets beyond: a kitchen.

We stepped in, and I found a switch on the wall. With a quick flick there was no need for a flashlight anymore. We didn't stop to check the cabinets. The kitchen had two other doors. I went left. The detective went right. I crouched and poked my head around the corner. A dingy, half-finished room ran back the length of the basement. It was being used for storage. Shelves of all kinds lived here: metal shelves, wooden shelves cobbled together from scrap lumber, plastic shelves bought at a Home Depot and hastily assembled. I didn't see any people.

I found the light switch and flicked it on. Stacked on the shelves were assorted boxes containing various electronics: laptops, game consoles, cell phones. Other items included automotive parts, random instruments, sculptures and art deco pieces. Nothing was in the original box. It was all stolen. A thief lived here. That was for sure.

I tracked around and between the shelves but didn't find anyone hiding out. I went back to the kitchen to the other door. Through it was a small bathroom, kept fairly tidy, and still another door which led to a bedroom.

The detective was bent over a body sprawled across a double bed. He had one knee on the mattress, checking vitals. I stopped in the doorway. I couldn't see who was on the bed.

"Dead?" I asked.

"Nah, just passed out," he replied.

I nodded. "There's something you should see."

"What's that?"

"Stolen goods. Lots of them."

The detective straightened. When he did, I could

see the person passed out on the bed. I took a deep breath and let it out, long and slow. It wasn't my mystery thief after all. That was for damn sure.

I figured Ronnie might have been short for Rhonda or maybe Veronica. The figure lying on the bed was a wiry woman with wild blonde hair. She wore skinny hip-hugger jeans and a black t-shirt a size too small. A half-empty bottle of Jack Daniels rested on the nightstand next to her. She was out cold.

Since she wouldn't be going anywhere soon, I directed the detective to the storage room on the other side of the apartment. After a quick perusal, he came back to the bedroom and cuffed the woman. She flopped around like a rag doll and stirred in her sleep but didn't wake up.

"I need to call this in," he said.

He stepped out of the basement, presumably to make a phone call and came back a few minutes later. Back-up was on the way, he said. We poked around the apartment while we waited, taking stock of all the stolen merchandise and shot the shit.

He'd been on the job just shy of eight years and made detective two years ago. His name was Sam. He seemed like a decent guy and a decent cop.

I told him about my investigation, the missing arti-fact, and that I'd considered Ronnie a person of interest, especially when I saw the stolen stuff, right up until I saw she was a woman. From what I'd seen in the video—the height, weight, and body composition—it was clear that my thief was most definitely male. Of course, that didn't mean she wouldn't have any useful information for me. The fact that she worked at the garage and my guy had worn a jacket with its logo was too big a coincidence to ignore. Maybe they knew each other. Maybe he was her boyfriend and had borrowed her jacket.

Sam told me that Ronnie had been a suspected thief for several months, but there wasn't enough evidence to arrest her. A car had been posted outside on and off for the last week to keep an eye on things, but nothing had come of it. He was glad I came along when I did, because now he had the evidence needed. Because of my fortuitous timing, he was happy to let me stick around and ask her some questions before hauling her down to the station.

The back-up arrived fifteen minutes later in the form of a single patrol car. Two officers got out and entered the apartment to secure the scene. It was another half-hour before Ronnie could be roused.

She was still somewhat drunk. I wondered just how long ago she had finished her binge. But it wouldn't be long before the hangover set in. Sam hung out in the bedroom doorway while I sat on the foot of the bed. Ronnie's head wobbled as she tried to watch me.

"Afternoon, Ronnie," I said. She just looked at me. "Your friends at the shop gave me your address."

"Iss my day off," she said, her words slurring to-gether.

"I can see that. Listen, the reason I need to talk to you is that something very important has gone missing."

She blinked at that, then bobbed and bobbled as she leaned closer.

"A lot of things go missing when I'm around," she whispered. Then she winked at me.

I resisted the urge to toss a look at Sam and roll my eyes. Instead, I said, "I can imagine. But I don't think you had anything to do with this one. I know it was a man who took it. Maybe you know who he is."

"Well, how should I know who did it if it wasn't me?"

"He was wearing a jacket like yours. One from the shop." She scrunched her face up in confusion.

"Was it your boyfriend?"

"Boyfriend?" she spat. "Men are pigs."

"No boyfriend, then."

"Nah, I don't swing that way," she said.

This conversation was definitely not going the di-rection I expected. "Okay. So where is your jacket?"

"I dunno. Work, maybe. I don't wear it."

Damn. This was looking like a dead end. I needed to switch trains, come at this from a different angle. "For-get the jacket, then. Who do you sell your stuff to?"

"What stuff?"

I gave her a flat look and she grinned at me. "It's looking like you're in a lot of trouble here. Do yourself a favor and help me out."

"Yeah, yeah. Depends on what stuff. There's a couple of guys."

I thought for a minute. She had a point. A whole spectrum of criminals participated in the black market. The pawnshop owner that bought electronics would sell to a different kind of person than someone who dealt in rare Syrian artifacts. That kind of fence would most likely have "clients." He would consider himself white-collar. Maybe he was an art dealer or purveyor of fine antiques. Something like that. He was still a scumbag.

"What about your sculptures and art pieces?" I asked.

She said nothing.

"Help me, help yourself."

"Arnie. He runs a second-hand store up on Foster." Then she went quiet and refused to say anything else.

Sam hauled her to her feet and half dragged her out to the street and loaded her into the back of his car. I followed them out, thanked him, and set off on foot.

Since I was looking for a fence, I figured I should give Brenda a call, finally, and see what she had learned.

"I had no idea this sort of thing even existed," Brenda said over the phone.

"What did you find out?"

"Okay, I'll try to keep it simple if I can, but I saved a bunch of articles for you to read when you have the time. First, the market for looted and illegally traded antiquities from the Middle East has exploded in the last ten years. There was a big scandal recently about some big arts and crafts store that had gotten involved, but they were shut down and the stuff confiscated. Sales of these items often go to fund terrorist organizations, which you would think would make Americans think twice about buying them, but apparently that's not the case."

"Okay, so there's an active market. Lots of stuff out there. How do buyers and sellers connect with each other?"

"Facebook."

"Seriously?"

"Seriously. There are groups that you can become a member of that help make those connections. There are other online avenues, too. What's surprising is that even reputable auction houses participate. As long as no one can prove the items were acquired illegally, they don't care."

"Are there any of those places around here?"

"Not that I've found. But there are so many mom and pop auctions and antique stores, it would be hard to tell. They don't exactly advertise."

"Right."

"One more thing. It seems that museums and universities aren't above acquiring these things either. Some try harder to verify the provenance of items, but others feel the protection they can offer is for the greater good."

"Interesting," I said, wondering if Dr. Halgrave had been completely honest with me. "Thanks. Keep digging. I'd love to know about the local market."

"Sure thing," she said, and we got off the phone.

I found Arnie's place easily enough. A quick google search over a whopper at Burger King told me it was at Foster and Kedzie, a bit of a hike from Ronnie's, but within thirty minutes.

The front windows of the store were crammed full of antiques: cherry wood dressers, silver trays, china sets. Inside, the clutter was worse. Piles of antiques, collectibles, and memorabilia littered the old concrete floor with moth-eaten Persian rugs and aisle runners covering up the exposed real estate.

An older gentleman with white tufts of hair ringing an otherwise shiny scalp rummaged around in the back of the store. Gold wire-rimmed glasses kept slipping down his nose as I approached.

"You Arnie?" I asked.

"Depends on who's asking," he replied with a smile.

"What's the oldest thing you have in here?"

He looked thoughtful for a moment, then said, "I've got some coins go back to the 1800's. That old enough?"

I shook my head. "I have something a lot older than that I'm looking to get rid of. I was told you're the guy to see about old stuff."

"Yes and no," he said. "I have a few customers with a taste for a certain era that I keep an eye out for. What have you got?"

"A vase," I lied. "Ming Dynasty."

He whistled low and shook his head. "That's a little out of my league. My customers can't afford museum quality pieces unless you're looking to sell really cheap."

"Not that cheap. Know anybody else I could talk to. If so, I'm sure a finder's fee would be in order."

His eyes lit up at that, but he didn't answer immediately. He was searching a mental Rolodex. Then he said, "Not off the top of my head. I could make some calls, though."

I scribbled my number on the back of one his business cards and left.

Evening was settling in. It was getting colder and clouds were scudding in across the sky. It felt like it was gearing up for a good snow. I shrugged the collar of my coat up higher and trudged on, heading toward the train.

I walked fast and thought hard.

Half a day's work had netted me nothing new. There was a connection to the auto shop; I was sure of that. Ronnie's place had been hopeful, but Arnie was a bust. I doubted he had access to the circle of crooks I needed. But something wasn't sitting right. A niggling feeling in the back of my brain told me that I was missing something.

Was it pure coincidence that there was another thief amidst the rank and file of Lon's Auto? The numbers said it was possible. Two and half million people lived in the city and there were roughly 74,000 reported thefts. Using the Pareto principle, or the 80/20 rule, eighty percent of those thefts were committed by twenty percent of all thieves living here. So roughly 60,000. That left 14,000 thefts to spread among the other eighty percent. A conservative estimate would be that those were done by 7,000 people which makes a total of about 8,750 people in an area of 234 square miles. If they were evenly distributed, that would mean thirty-seven people per square mile. Of course, we all know that distribution is nowhere near even, but Albany Park sees an average amount of crime. Which meant there were a total of seventy-four potential bad guys in the neighborhood. It wouldn't be at all implausible that two of them worked at the same auto shop. The more I thought about it, the more likely it actually seemed.

But that niggling feeling wouldn't go away. Maybe it wasn't coincidence. Maybe the two were connected somehow. But how? I couldn't see it. I needed to take a break.

The wind picked up as I got to the train station where I made a last-minute phone call. By the time I was halfway to downtown, snow was flying.

14

The sky was turning the steel gray of a winter evening as the thief hustled down the sidewalk. He was no ordinary thief, however. He was a master thief. There was none better. There was nothing he couldn't steal, and he'd never been caught. Over the years, he'd taken fewer and fewer jobs because he didn't need the money and it held no thrill for him anymore. The only jobs he took were ones that held some personal value for him or were for a good cause which is why he occupied himself with other interests, vocations that presented a challenge.

This evening was different. A dial tone purred in his ear as the cellphone he held tried to make a connection. Four rings, then five, and no one picked up.

He glanced around for the fifteenth time to make sure he wasn't being followed. It wasn't something that normally concerned him. He had a way of moving unseen along the tree-lined streets when he wanted to. It was just like the way he could get in and out of any location without being spotted, which is why he was never caught. It was an innate ability, one that required no thought. When he had thought about it, however, it was mostly to wonder how it worked. The best he could figure was that it sprung from a subconscious understanding of eyelines and fields of view, calculating angles of approach and vectors of movement that allowed him to be virtually invisible.

The phone purred on. Seven rings. Eight. On the tenth, someone picked up.

"Yes," said a voice like old parchment rustling under a scribe's fingertips.

"I'm out," said the thief.

"Why?"

"He's close."

"Who?"

"The detective. No one has ever been this close before. If my involvement is discovered, I'm dead." The thief's voice pitched higher as he spoke. He hadn't been this nervous in ages.

There was a pause as the man on the other end considered the new information. "We will deal with the detective," the papery voice finally said. "Your continued involvement is greatly appreciated. It displays a measure of goodwill that will be returned in kind. Lie low for a while if you wish but stay close."

The line went dead.

The thief blew out a long breath and watched the cloud of fog it created. He slipped the phone back in his pocket and picked up the pace. His employer might not be worried yet, but the fact that the detective had gotten this close already spoke volumes about Gray's skills and that added an unanticipated and unwelcome element of danger to the arrangement.

If his employer could get rid of the threat, so be it. If

not, he would relocate—maybe to California. The weather there was a lot better than Chicago.

He refocused on his surroundings and slid through the shadows like a ghost. Ten minutes later, he unlocked the door to his apartment and began to pack. "Three days," he whispered to himself. "Three days and then I'm gone."

15

I went all the way downtown to Michigan Avenue. From Thanksgiving on, it's lit up and decorated for the holiday season—a majestic place. Though I haven't had a reason to shop for years, I always enjoyed the atmosphere.

This year, though, I had people to buy for. With Frank gone, I considered it my responsibility to see that the girls had a decent Christmas. It wouldn't be good, of course, not the first one without their dad, but I could make an effort.

The problem was, I didn't have a clue what to get. Fortunately, that created the perfect opportunity for a second date. Stacy met me at the Cheesecake Factory in Water Tower Place for dinner and accompanied me to all the big stores afterward. She had a pretty good handle on what was in at the moment, and though we steered clear of clothing, there were plenty of techno gadgets and make-up and accessories that would delight all the girls. Our conversation stayed on the light side. I made corny jokes. Stacy smiled and rolled her eyes simultaneously. I could tell I was winning her over with my abundant charm.

Three hours later, I had an armful of entirely too expensive merchandise that I hoped someone would appreciate. My good cheer was also thoroughly spent, but the night wasn't over yet.

As we walked along the brightly lit Magnificent Mile, Stacy said, "I was hoping you would do me a favor."

"What's that?"

"Would you be willing to let me take a blood sample? I'd like to run some tests."

I watched her out of the corner of my eye. Did I want to be her guinea pig? Part of me didn't want to be anyone's pet project, but it wasn't like she was asking for a kidney. My gut told me I could trust her. And I, of all people, understood her desire to solve a puzzle. Maybe she would find some answers, a scientific explanation for my accelerated healing.

"Yeah, okay," I said.

We took a cab back to her apartment in Greektown, not far from the Loop. She lived on the eighth floor of a new high-rise and I was looking forward to seeing it. Condo living was outside my realm of experience. It probably had a nice view of downtown. Maybe not the best, only being on the eighth floor, but better than what I had from my apartment.

It was well after dark when we arrived, and the snow was coming down hard. The cab dropped us off at the front entrance. We walked through the revolving doors into a well-lit lobby with high ceilings and hardwood floors. It was strung with white lights and decked with elegant seasonal decor. A doorman or possibly a concierge stood behind a slim counter and nodded at us. To the right was a lounge area with several plush chairs and end tables. To the left was a short hallway with a bank of elevators. We went left, but Stacy walked right past the elevators. She didn't even hit the call button.

Beyond the elevators was a set of glass doors. All was dark on the other side. I followed Stacy because I had no idea where we were going. She withdrew a set of keys from her purse and used one of them to unlock the doors and pushed them open. She held it for me as I stepped through.

Once inside, I realized this was the commercial part of the building, kind of like a small mall, and contained a number of retail locations. It wasn't actually as dark as it appeared due to several lights left burning in a few stores and ambient light from outside filtering in.

Stacy locked the door behind her and led me through the vacant space to another door. Above it, a big white and red sign proclaimed it was an emergi-care facility—one of those places where well-insured people go to see a doctor when they don't feel like making an appointment three weeks after they're sick. She unlocked this door as well which led into yet another warren of hallways and exam rooms.

"I moonlight here when I'm not at the hospital. The pay is better, and I don't have to go far from home," she said.

I nodded as she opened an exam room door and turned on the light. I started to sit on the exam table, but she told me to have a seat in the chair next to it instead. She said I'd be more comfortable, and she wouldn't feel like I was just a patient. Then she left the room. I took off my coat, draped it across the back of the chair, and rolled up my sleeves.

A few minutes later, she came back with a handful of supplies and laid them out on the counter beside the chair.

"So," I said as she swabbed my arm down with alcohol. "What are you hoping to find?"

She felt around the soft part of my forearm and said, "I'm not sure, really. An anomaly in your DNA to explain the healing factor would be ideal but maybe there's something else." She found a vein and looked up at me. "Thanks for indulging me." Then she jabbed me with the needle.

I've never been fond of needles. Actually, I hate them. Abhor them, even. One time when I was a kid and had to get a shot for school, it took three nurses to hold me down. I've gotten a little better about it over the years, and my time in the hospital gave me the opportunity to get used to them, but I still have a deeply rooted fear of needles. I'm not afraid of much else, but the sight of a hypodermic syringe gives me the heebie-jeebies. It was everything I could do to sit there without squirming.

Or crying.

I focused on my breathing and let myself slide into...what? The Nether? The Void? I needed to come up with a suitable name for whatever the other place was where the strange energies existed. Reality blurred, shifted, and the swirling lights came into focus. I didn't look at them directly. Instead, I focused on nothing and everything at once. A moment later, Stacy removed the needle, placing a cotton ball over the insertion point, and smiled at me. I looked back at her; watched the soft threads of light seep from her skin. Part of me wanted to reach out and touch them. I almost did, but I stopped myself. Tapping into energy coming directly out of a person might not be the best idea, but I wanted to show her what I could do.

I reached down and lifted the cotton ball from my arm. Blood welled up around the puncture. "Watch," I told her, and I reached out for a different strand of white light nearby. I willed the connection to happen and the light flowed up my arm. Immediately, the tiny wound closed itself. I broke the connection and wiped the blood away with the cotton ball, showing her the result as I slid back to reality.

"I have to concentrate to make it happen," I told her. She watched me closely, but I couldn't read her expression. Was it awe? Surprise? Suspicion? Maybe all of them wrapped into a big ball of confusion.

"It's remarkable," she said.

I nodded and looked at my arm. My phone started ringing then. I checked the caller id and saw that it was a blocked number, so I ignored it.

"How do you do it?" she asked.

I shook my head. "It sounds crazy," I told her.

My phone started ringing again. I checked it again. It read "unavailable." I ignored it again and put it back in my pocket.

"It is crazy," she said. "But it's happening. I just saw it. If I told another doctor, they'd think I was crazy, too."

I let out a deep breath, thinking it over, making a decision. Then my phone rang again. "Dammit," I said as I pulled the phone out once more. It still said "unavailable" but I hit the button anyway. "What?" I said into the phone.

"Mr. Gray?" said a thin, papery voice.

"Yes. Who is this? What do you want?"

"I'm sorry to bother you at such a late hour, but I have some information that you might find valuable."

It sounded like a typical telemarketer line, but there was something in his voice that kept me from hanging up. "What kind of information?"

"Regarding a certain item you are looking for," the voice said.

That got my attention. "I'm listening."

"As I said, you might find it valuable. I'd like to discuss just how valuable."

"I suppose that depends on the nature of the information," I said.

Stacy had gone quiet. I looked at her apologetically. She shrugged and peeled a barcoded label from a sheet and stuck it to the vial of blood.

"I have a location," said the man on the phone.

"How did you come by this information?" I asked.

"I have a wide network of business associates. Information is a commodity I trade in on a regular basis. It was brought to my attention that you are looking for said information."

"Okay," I said.

"The question now is: how much is it worth to you?"

"It's not worth anything at the moment," I told him.

"Really?"

"Really. I have no idea who you are. I have no idea if your information is valid. I certainly have no reason to trust you. You could be some con artist looking for a quick score."

"I see," he said. There was a long pause. I figured he was thinking about his next move. "Fair enough," he finally said. "Because we have never done business before, I need to prove the authenticity of what I offer. Unfortunately, information is not simply an item that can be examined before a transaction is made. Which puts me in a difficult position."

"Not my problem," I said.

"However, I believe you have the potential to be a profitable customer in the future and worth an initial investment. I will tell you what I know freely in hopes that a working relationship can be established."

"Kind of like a free trial? If what you tell me checks out, next time you'll want payment up front?"

"Something like that, yes."

"Fair enough. So, what do you know?"

"An item fitting the description of the one you seek has temporarily come into the possession of a high-end art dealer." This seemed to be exactly the kind of thing Brenda had told me about.

"I see. How long will it be in this person's possession?"

"Two days at most. After that, I have no idea where it will be."

"Okay, what's the address?" Stacy handed me a pen without being asked and I jotted down the location he gave me. "Thanks. If this checks out, I'll owe you. How can I contact you?" I asked.

"You can't," he said. "If I have anything that might interest you in the future, I'll contact you. I have your number." Then the call was disconnected, and all I heard was silence on the other end.

"What was that about?" Stacy asked.

"The case I'm working on. Someone just gave me some very helpful information." I thought about Arnie. The last thing he said was he'd make some calls. Maybe he had. I narrowed my eyes, thinking it over.

"What's wrong?" Stacy asked again.

"I don't know," I admitted. "Something about that call isn't sitting right." Sitting right or not, I needed to check it out. I looked at Stacy. "Thanks for helping me out tonight," I said.

"It was fun. Thanks for asking me."

There was a moment of awkward silence. Part of me didn't want the evening to end, but another part wanted to get back to work.

Stacy must have been thinking the same thing because she finally said, "Well."

"Yeah," I said. "I should get going."

"I'll walk you out."

I put my coat on and gathered up all the packages. Stacy led me back to the lobby of the building and paused at the doors. Before I realized what was happening, she stood on her tiptoes and kissed me on the cheek. I felt my face flush and mumbled something unintelligible.

Stacy smiled and said, "See you soon?"

"Count on it," I replied before making my exit.

16

I took a cab home and spent the duration of the trip researching the art gallery where the mysterious caller said the artifact was being held. According to him, it would be there for two days, but I didn't want to risk it being moved early.

The gallery closed at eight and wouldn't reopen until ten the next morning. That left me with two options: I could head over tonight, break in, and see what I could find or I could wait until morning and go as a potential buyer. The first option would be tricky. A high-end art gallery probably had a high-end security system. I might be able to pick locks but getting past motion sensors and alarm codes is well beyond my capabilities. If I waited until the morning, I wouldn't have to worry about that. Instead, I'd have to figure out how to snoop around without any of the staff becoming suspicious.

Of course, there was also the possibility of the whole thing being a trap. How somebody had figured out that I was investigating the theft in the first place rubbed me the wrong way. I hadn't told anybody other than the people at the museum. It was possible the robbery was an inside job, which was how they knew. Maybe they wanted to get rid of me. Going in at night would give them that opportunity. I opted to wait.

I had an idea, though, so I made a phone call.

"Hello?" said Dr. Halgrave.

"Good evening, Dr. Halgrave," I began.

"Meredith, please.

"Right. I'm sorry to bother you so late, but I got a phone call earlier this evening that might interest you."

"Really?"

"Yeah. Someone claims that your artifact is being held at an art gallery in the East Village."

"That's wonderful," she said, her voice bubbling at the good news.

"Maybe," I warned. "I don't know if it's legit. Something feels hinky about it. I'm going to check it out, but I could use your help. I don't really know what this thing looks like up close. You could verify its authenticity." I didn't tell her that I also wanted her there to help me blend in. I don't really look like the kind of guy that goes to an art gallery. Plus, she would make an excellent distraction—assuming the purveyor was interested in women, maybe even if they weren't.

"Oh, I would love to help," she cooed.

"Good. What kind of car do you have?"

"A Lexus."

"Perfect. Would you be willing to pick me up at my office at nine tomorrow morning?"

"Of course. I'll wear something appropriate as well. See you then."

We clicked off the call, and I let out a deep breath.

Just talking to her on the phone made my stomach do somersaults. I wasn't sure how I would manage to play it cool tomorrow. It was late and I was tired. I looked around the apartment and spotted Willy perched on the back of the couch.

"We need to talk," I said, then shook my head at how ridiculous that sounded. Not that it was any more ridiculous than healing myself with blue lights, but still. After a quick shower, I crawled into bed and was asleep in minutes.

***

"So, talk," the old man said. We were on a mountain top overlooking a deep valley, lush with the green of a pristine coniferous forest. Water shimmered far below. I'd never seen anything like it.

"I have questions," I said.

He nodded.

I thought about which one to ask first. "What am I?"

"A detective, I presume," he said.

It was a flippant answer, and I almost said something snarky in reply but stopped myself. He was right. I was a detective. It was the single biggest part of what defined me. Ever since I was a kid, mysteries and puzzles drew me in, demanding to be solved. And I was good at it. When I worked for the Department, there were rumors that the Feds were looking at me for recruitment. The FBI most likely, and it would have been fine with me. But it was only a matter of time before it all blew up anyway.

I was too impatient. The wheels of the justice system creep at a snail's pace. There are too many barriers to allow a detective to do his job efficiently. The private sector fit me a lot better. I was pretty happy where I ended up, though I did miss catching the bad guys. So whatever else I was, the old man was right. I was a detective first.

"What else?" I finally asked.

"Many things," he replied. "As are we all. But you know this already."

I said nothing. My brain was trying to come up with the right question.

After a moment, a breath escaped him and carried sounds with it, but they were foreign to me. "Skyggekriger."

"Pardon?" I looked at him blankly.

"That is what your kind was called where I came from. Roughly translated, it means Shadow Warrior, but I have heard others say Shadow Walker. You have the ability to see and use the Skygge, the in-between place where those lights you see exist."

"Shadow Walker," I repeated. "That sounds about right." Then I asked, "So what are you?"

He didn't answer immediately. Instead, he gazed across the landscape for a long minute. When he finally spoke, his voice was softer than I'd heard before, full of wistfulness. "I used to come here when I needed to think. But that was a long time ago. It has probably changed so much, I wouldn't recognize it now.

"But that is the nature of life, is it not? Nothing is constant but change. The fabric of who we are is always in flux. As our experience and perspectives change, so do we." He looked at me then with a wry smile on his cracked lips.

I said nothing.

"Listen to me prattle on about existential philosophy." He snorted. "My apologies. I am not normally prone to such discourse. Perhaps it is my age or want of discerning company that brings it out. But what I said is true. I have been many things over the years, and it can be easy to forget what I truly am.

"You could best call me a Dreamwalker, I suppose. That is what I do, and I think is most directly related to what you meant to ask."

"A Dreamwalker?"

"Yes. I am able to project my consciousness into another's mind while they sleep. More importantly, I can control those dreams, make you see and hear whatever I desire."

"How is that possible?" I asked.

He shrugged. "I do not know. There are still many mysteries yet to be solved. The workings of the human mind are perhaps the greatest of them all."

"So, you can only talk to me if I'm asleep?"

"I can only access a semi-conscious or uncon-scious mind. Sleep is the most common way, but there are others."

"What happens when I wake up?"

"Essentially, I get kicked out. Though if the mind is weak enough or simple enough, I can take over."

That gave me a moment's pause.

"But you don't need to worry about that. I couldn't hitch a ride in your conscious mind if I tried."

We went quiet after that. Sitting still on the moun-tain, both of us lost in thought.

17

I was at the office by seven-thirty. Dr. Halgrave would be by to get me soon, and I had a few other items of business to tend to. I turned my attention to the other investigation on my mind. Conrad told me the McCarthy case was put on the back burner after being dumped on by his lieutenant, one Donald Wiggins. I didn't know much about him, but that was about to change. First, I read through all of the reports I already had, looking for his name. It appeared in a few places, but strictly in an administrative capacity.

I could call Larsen to see what he could give me on the guy, but it probably wouldn't be much. Larsen wasn't high enough up the food chain or in the right department to have access to his personnel file. Instead, I did some digital sleuthing to dig into Wiggins's personal life. I had his home phone number, street address, email address, and driving record within minutes. Beyond that, I didn't turn up much of anything. He had no social media footprint, no traffic offenses or open court cases, and google didn't give me anything useful in the first two pages of search results. I'd investigated people with less information available, but not by much.

I leaned back in the chair and considered my options. Internal Affairs didn't care much for me, so I doubted they'd take any inquiries seriously. Jack could probably give me the scuttlebutt but not much else.

I'd have to cast my net a little wider. There were other contacts I could call on. It was eight o'clock and he just might be in by now. I looked up the information I needed and dialed the phone. Someone picked up after the third ring. "Good morning, Alderman Juarez's office," the cheerful voice said. "How may I serve you today?"

"Good morning." I said back. "I'd like to speak with Mr. Juarez, please."

"May I ask who's calling, please?"

"This is Detective Gray. I worked on a case for him not long ago." Politicians rarely speak with members of their constituency at a moment's notice, but he was Ellie McCarthy's fiancé. Ultimately, it was his fault I'd gone looking under the right rock to find her and found a whole lot of trouble to boot. But he was extremely grateful I had done so, going so far as to say he owed me one. That was a pretty big deal, coming from somebody like him. So I was pretty sure he'd take my call.

"Hold please," the receptionist said. The phone clicked and horrible music poured out of the handset. I waited patiently for a minute or two, before the receptionist came back on the line. "I'm sorry Mr. Gray. The Alderman is in a meeting at the moment and can't take your call, but he asked me to take a message if there is one, and he'll return your call as soon as possible."

"Alright. Tell him I have some information regarding our prior case that he might find interesting. I'll be in the office until nine. If I don't hear from him by then, I'll call back when I'm free.

"Very good. I'll let him know. Have a nice day."

Brenda was there by the time I hung up. She gave me the articles she'd printed out the day before and I started to peruse them. Before I got very far, the phone rang. It was Alderman Juarez.

"Detective," he said when I picked up. "How are you?"

"Better than I deserve, I suppose. How's Ellie?"

"Good. She's recovered quite well, though the ordeal has set our engagement plans back a bit."

"Understandable."

"You said you had some information for me." One thing I like about Juarez is that he says what's on his mind. Another politician might have talked around the topic for an hour before getting down to business.

"Remember how suspicious you were about Ellie's case? You thought somebody wasn't taking it seriously."

"Yes," he said tentatively.

"I have confirmation of that. I spoke with the lead detective. He was told to assign priority to other cases. Essentially, his commander told him not to waste his time with it."

"Why?"

"I don't know yet, but I'm working on it. I could

use your help, though."

"What do you need?" His tone turned serious.

"The officer in charge was a Lieutenant Donald Wiggins. I've done some digging on my end but haven't found anything useful. What I'd really like to see are his case files and ones he's supervised. I'm not interested in the successful ones at the moment. I think the evidence will be in the cold cases. I don't have access to that kind of information and calling in favors from my contacts in the department might raise some flags, maybe alert him that he's being watched. I'd like to avoid that."

There was silence on the other end of the line as Juarez considered. Then, "I'll see what I can do."

***

Dr. Halgrave called me from her car at precisely nine o'clock. I bundled up, carted myself down the front stairs and stepped out the door. A sleek, white Lexus, all sexy curves and only slightly crusted with the grime and salt of the city streets, was double parked on the far curb.

The driver's side window buzzed down as I approached. "Get in," Dr. Halgrave said. Her voice was smooth and silky and threatened to melt me despite the freezing temperature.

I stepped around to the passenger side, popped the handle, and slid inside. Warm air greeted me, and another warm feeling blanketed me when I saw Dr. Halgrave's smile.

167

"Where to?" she asked, and I wondered if she had any idea of the effect she was having on me.

I gave her the address and tried to make small talk as we drove along the streets, made narrow by mounting snow that had been plowed to the sides. She was perfectly comfortable. I, however, grew more flustered with each passing minute. I caught her up on the details of the case so far. She was particularly interested in the mystery man caught on tape and pelted me with questions about my visit to the auto shop.

When we got to the East Village, we found a parking spot two blocks from the gallery and climbed out of the car. As soon as the cold air hit me, I snapped out of whatever stupor I'd been in and started thinking straight again. There was something strange about Dr. Halgrave. The thought surprised me. Why hadn't I noticed it before? Or had I?

By the time she stepped up onto the sidewalk next to me, I had forgotten all about it. She offered her arm to me and I stared at it, not understanding.

"To keep up appearances," she said. Then it dawned on me. I had asked her along to help me fit in. She was offering to play the part of the wealthy wife interested in art while I would be the unobtrusive husband with no interest whatsoever. All of which suited me fine. In the back of my brain, a little voice told me that was what I had intended all along. I stuck my elbow out and she hooked her arm through it.

The gallery was in the second floor of a 1970's era red brick loft. A small sign hanging from the side of the building was the only indication of its presence. I guess it was one of those pretentious places that didn't advertise, instead relying on word of mouth and its reputation to bring in a select handful of customers who would spend exorbitant amounts of money on one-of-a-kind pieces.

A single glass door led from the street to a flight of wooden stairs, worn smooth from years of use. We followed the stairs up to the second floor which opened into a wide space with a twelve-foot-high vaulted ceiling. The interior plaster walls had been removed, leaving the brick, ductwork, and plumbing exposed, giving the place an industrial feel. A single white wall of newly installed sheetrock bisected the loft. It was only a partial wall, not reaching the top of the ceiling, but sufficient enough to create a separate space, probably used for offices and storage.

A variety of paintings hung on the walls. There were landscapes and still lifes, abstracts and cubism. Sculptures of diverse materials and composition dotted the floor. Some were metal monstrosities that I doubted could be removed from the gallery without demolishing an entire wall. Others were more manageable, crafted from wood, stone, and clay. Some were clearly modern, while others could have been ancient.

We were greeted immediately by a tall thin gentleman wearing a suit that must have cost a thousand dollars—maybe from Brooks Brothers. It definitely wasn't from Men's Warehouse. A garish pink paisley tie delicately nestled in the "v" of his vest. His gaze flowed over us, calculating our net worth, no doubt. A tiny frown pulled the corners of his mouth downward as his eyes slid over me. When they came to rest on Dr. Halgrave, a half smile returned.

"Good afternoon," he said. "My name is Andrew Vicars. How can I serve you today?"

Dr. Halgrave smiled at him—that beautiful, genuine, disarming smile she'd given me the first time we met that caused my stomach to do somersaults and my legs turn to jelly. I could see something similar was happening to Andrew.

"A close, personal friend of mine recommended your gallery," Halgrave said. "She said you have some exquisite pieces, and I'm about to redo our sitting room so I'm looking for something exquisite to be the focal point."

Andrew never looked at me again. He was completely enthralled from that point on. They continued their conversation, which I couldn't follow at all, and began drifting around the gallery from piece to piece. I assumed they discussed the qualities of each, the pros and cons, but honestly, I wasn't paying attention.

At one point, Dr. Halgrave had her phone out

while she was talking. Then my own phone buzzed. She'd
sent me a picture of the stolen artifact and a text saying:
Go look. I've got this.

18

I wandered away from the pair, plastering a bored expression on my face and meandered toward a door in the center wall. It was closed, but not locked. I waited until their backs were turned and slipped through, closing the door behind me.

A corridor ran directly ahead for about fifty feet and ended at a window overlooking the back of the building. Three doors were evenly spaced along the left-hand side, and one was placed in the center of the right side. I eased down the hallway and checked the first door on the left. It was slightly ajar, so I peeked in. A simple office lay on the other side. A desk, a chair, a computer, and a file cabinet. Nothing else.

The door on the right was a different story. It was closed and locked. A quick assessment told me I could pick it, but I hadn't brought my tools. I wanted to make sure the rest of the place was clear before breaking into a locked room, so I decided I'd come back to it.

The second room was larger than the office. It was a kitchenette. A long counter lined the far wall and contained a sink. A coffee pot and microwave were lined up side by side. In the center of the room was a long table lined with chairs. Art hung on the walls. I guessed this was where the sales pitches and negotiations happened.

The far door was also locked. I heard movement

on the other side. Because I hadn't seen one yet, I figured there was a bathroom behind it. I stood patiently and waited. Several minutes later, the door opened and a large man stepped out, wiping his hands on black slacks. He wasn't dressed as nicely as Andrew—just the slacks and a white shirt with the sleeves rolled up—and he had a broad, ugly face. Not a face for public consumption. A backroom guy. Maybe a partner, maybe a buyer, but not a salesman. Or maybe, if this place was dealing in the black market, he was the muscle.

He jerked up straight when he saw me and grunted. He looked me up and down then stepped aside so I could enter the bathroom, which I did. After the door closed, I heard his heavy footsteps retreat down the hallway. I counted off thirty seconds in my head then flushed and turned on the faucet and let the water run for ten seconds before shutting it off. I opened the door and stepped back in the hall. Nobody waited for me.

I peeked into the kitchen again to make sure it was empty, then went back to the locked center door. I used the same trick I had at Ronnie's, slipping into the Skygge and grabbing a little extra strength, felt my pulse quicken and adrenaline spike, then turned the doorknob hard. It snicked as the locking mechanism sheared off and I stepped through.

On the other side was a storage space that ran the full length of the subdivided room, rectangular in shape, roughly fifty feet by twenty. Eight racks designed to hold stretched canvases and half a dozen shelves were arranged neatly around the floor. I didn't have time to take a closer look.

Ten feet from the door sat the man from the bathroom, rocked back on two legs of a metal folding chair. He was staring at a phone in his hand. Light reflected off his broad face as whatever he watched flashed from one image to the next. He looked up as I entered. When he saw me, he let the front two chair legs hit the floor and stood up in one smooth motion.

"You lost?" he asked in an eastern European accent. Maybe Ukrainian. Maybe Polish.

"No," I said. "I think I'm right where I'm supposed to be."

I must have confused him because he said, "What?"

"I think you have something for me."

He shook his head. "No. I have nothing for you."

"I think you do."

He shook his head again. "Leave now."

By this point I was certain the guy was hired muscle. He was here to protect something—probably the stolen goods. He wasn't going to stand there and let me poke around. But that's exactly what I wanted to do. I had a choice to make. Either I walked away and lost the only chance I had to see if the artifact was actually here, or I dealt with this guy quickly without getting hurt in the process. I chose the latter.

He was a big guy and probably had a lot of experience hurting people. Intimidation wasn't going to work with him. I had to hit him hard and fast. I took a step forward and put my hands in front of me, palms out.

"I'm sorry," I said and took another step. Almost there. "I'm supposed to pick up an item. Andrew said it was back here and that you would make sure I got the right one."

His eyes flicked right, away from the door, toward something, but I didn't look to see what it was. Instead, I closed the rest of the distance between us in one stride and shot my right arm out, fingers bent, and jabbed him hard in the throat.

His hands went to his throat and he bent forward as he tried to suck in air through a rapidly swelling windpipe, so I followed up with an elbow to the temple. The lights went out and he toppled to the side.

I stooped down to check his pulse. It was there. He was still breathing, too, so no permanent damage done with the throat punch. He had a concussion for sure, but I wasn't about to sweat that. I turned my attention to the rest of the room, focusing on the direction Muscle Head had glanced. Since I'd just mentioned an item being picked up, odds were good that he'd looked at it just then.

To the right, sitting on a table against the back

wall, was a large fireproof safe. I hadn't seen it before, but I hadn't really looked all that closely. I moved over to give it a closer inspection. It was about two feet tall and eighteen inches wide. It looked heavy, too heavy to carry out of here. There was a grid of buttons on the front. I thought about tapping into the Skygge and trying to smash the thing, but then I'd probably destroy whatever was inside.

I looked back at Muscle Head lying on the floor. He didn't look like a very smart guy. Maybe he wasn't one for memorizing numbers. I stepped back over to his prone form and patted him down. A wallet was in his back pocket. I wriggled it out and flipped through it. He had a driver's license, two credit cards, eighty bucks in cash, and a small slip of folded paper. I ignored everything but the slip of paper, took it out, and carefully unfolded it. Bingo. Four numbers were written on it. I hustled back to the safe and punched them in on the keypad. It didn't open on the first try, so I tried again, pushing the buttons a little more carefully. This time, I was rewarded with a satisfying thunk when I pressed the ENTER key and the door popped open.

Using one finger, I swung the door wide and peered inside. Three stacks of hundred dollar bills sat inside which I eyed for a moment. Stealing from thieves wasn't exactly a moral quandary, but it was possible there were employees who needed to be paid. I decided against taking it. There were also several file folders inside, which didn't interest me, and a green velvet pouch about the size of a two-liter bottle that did. I reached in and removed the pouch. There was something solid inside. A black drawstring held the pouch closed. I carefully loosened the cord and peeked in. It was a statue, hewn of some dark brown stone, and only just resembled a person. It looked old, but I was no expert.

I took out my phone and thumbed open the text message Dr. Halgrave had sent me. I studied the picture closely and compared it to the statue in the the pouch. As far as I could tell, they were identical. Pulling the drawstrings closed again, I stuffed the whole package into my coat pocket and made a hasty retreat.

Out in the main gallery, Andrew was still in rapt conversation with Dr. Halgrave. I caught her eye as I came in and resumed a slow meander in their direction. I hoped she could wrap things up quickly. I really didn't want to be around when Muscle Head woke up. I doubted he'd be a very happy camper. I stepped up to the doctor's side and cleared my throat impatiently.

Halgrave glanced at me, then at the watch on her wrist. "I'm terribly sorry, Andrew," she said, laying a hand on his arm. "My husband has a meeting, and we really must be going. I'll have to tell Marguerite that she was right about you. I'll be in touch." She disengaged gently, took my arm, and smiled at Andrew as we went back down the stairs.

We played our parts out on the street until we were out of sight. Halgrave cranked the ignition and turned the heat all the way up while I extracted the green pouch from my pocket and loosened the cord. My fingers were cold, and I certainly didn't want to do any damage to it so I didn't do much more than pull the fabric down around the statue, like changing a sleeping baby's diaper.

Dr. Halgrave stared at it for a long moment. "I can't be sure until we get it back to the lab, she said. "But I think that's it. Well done."

There was sincere admiration in her voice, and my heart thumped against the inside of my ribcage hard enough I was sure she could hear it. She put the car in gear and pulled out into the street.

There was a quiet tension in the car. I could feel her excitement at having recovered whatever this thing was. I should have been happy about it too, but I wasn't. I tried to sift through my thoughts and pinpoint exactly why but kept getting distracted by the energy she was putting out.

Energy. Something about her energy.

I let myself slip into the Skygge and sucked in a quick breath of surprise at what I saw. Instead of the blue-white tendrils I was now used to seeing, Dr. Halgrave was giving off a yellow haze. It radiated from her in pulses before forming long tentacles of energy that snaked their way across the seat of the car and brushed against me with a soft caress. That shouldn't be happening. I checked my psychic faraday cage. It was still conducting the other red and blue ambient energy around me harmlessly, but the yellow stuff seemed to be probing my defenses, looking for a way in. It didn't flow like the rest. Instead, it felt like it was being directed.

I suddenly felt vulnerable and somehow violated, immediately throwing up a wall to keep the yellow fingers away. The energy recoiled and wrapped itself around her. She looked at me suddenly, the look on her face like she had just been slapped. Maybe I'd done the psychic equivalent. I had no idea.

My head cleared instantly, and I was able to think straight again. Good thing, too. I had a lot to think about now. I wasn't sure what had just happened or the significance of what I'd seen, but it would require serious scrutiny later. For now, though, I wanted to figure out what was bothering me about the artifact.

It took me ten long minutes to come up with an answer. The car was silent the entire time. No banter, no chit-chat like before. There was still tension, but it was different. And it was mostly on Dr. Halgrave's end.

"How will you authenticate it?" I finally asked.

Her face brightened a bit, and some of the tension went out of her, like she was relieved I'd spoken. "Visual comparison, mostly. We'll check it against a number of photos and take measurements. Our cataloging is pretty meticulous. We can also take a tiny sample and run it through mass spectrometry to make sure it has the same chemical composition."

"How long will it take?"

"Two days at minimum. A week at most."

I nodded but said nothing.

"What's wrong?" she asked.

"Nothing," I lied. "Just thinking."

We drove for another ten minutes before reaching the office. After we pulled up to the curb, I handed the velvet pouch across the seat. She laid her hand on mine and her touch felt electric, but I was better able to ignore it this time.

"Thank you again," she breathed. "Truly."

"Don't thank me yet," I told her. "Wait until the authentication comes back positive." I watched the kernel of doubt worm its way into her brain, her brows knitting together in response.

"Let's hope it does," I added before I opened the door and unfolded myself into the cold.

19

"What do you know about vampires?" I asked. I had largely ignored their existence since tangling with the two who had killed Frank at Navy Pier. They were dead, I wasn't. That part was over. Now, my time was better spent ferreting out the corruption in the police department. At least, that's what I told myself. The truth was I still didn't understand how they existed or why no one knew they did. Normally when I don't understand something, I investigate. People might think I was crazy, but the idea of investigating vampires seemed absurd. Now, with my Dreamwalker mentor, maybe it was time to embrace the absurd.

Willy looked at me and arched a bushy eyebrow. "Not much," he admitted.

"But you know they're for real?"

"Of course." He paused. "But they aren't like the stories. Those creatures are pure fiction."

"Right," I said. "No flying, no turning into bats, no coffins. But they do drink blood. They're incredibly strong and incredibly fast, and they heal extremely fast. I've seen that for myself."

"Seems like you know quite a bit about them already. What else were you hoping for?"

"Why haven't they taken over the world and turned us all into cattle?"

His eyebrow arched again. "Maybe they have."

I gave him a questioning look—not sure if he was being a smartass or being sincere. He was pretty good at being a smartass. Maybe better than me.

"There's something you need to understand. Mankind is not alone in this world. They never have been. Once upon a time, those of us born of the Skygge, and I include myself in that group, were well known to men."

"Born of the Skygge?" I interrupted.

"Beings like myself. Not human. What you might call the supernatural."

"Like me."

"No. You are different. You are human, but something else as well. You have one foot in your world and one in ours. I can't explain it better than that."

"I see."

"Now, as I was saying. In ancient days, some of the Shadow Born were revered as gods, some as demons. But mankind evolved quickly, hunted down those they feared, and put their faith in science. For all of our advantages, we are not invulnerable. Far from it. We had to adapt. Hide. Blend in. Some of us excelled at this. The rest perished.

"Imagine if everyone suddenly became aware of our existence today. With your technology, we would be eradicated completely. Our survival depends on secrecy. That being said, it is not impossible that some have blended in so well or become so adept at working from the shadows that they have infiltrated the highest levels of government or corporate management, thereby exerting their will onto the world once more."

Interesting. Also, terrifying. But on second thought, maybe not. Whatever their strengths, their biggest weakness was their need to go unseen. Which meant they had to operate like normal people.

"How many of you are there?"

"I do not know. It has been decades since I have encountered any others, but I live on the fringe, even for a Skygge Born."

I went quiet then, contemplating the implications of what he'd told me.

***

The doorbell rang while I was in the shower. It was nine in the morning and I was having a hard time getting started. I swore and twisted the handles to shut the water off before grabbing a thin yellow towel, wrapping it around my waist. Still dripping water, I hopped to the front door and looked through the peephole. A bike messenger stood on the landing outside. I unlocked the door and opened it an inch.

"Yeah?" I said, voice croaking.

"I've got a package for a Mr. Gray."

"Yeah, okay," I said and opened the door a little wider. The guy handed me a heavy brown accordion file

183

and a clipboard.

"If you could just sign here," he said.

I signed the paper on the clipboard and tossed the package on the couch in the living room before locking up and going back to the bathroom. Once I dried off and dressed, I went back to see what the package was about. The file was wrapped tightly with half a dozen thick rubber bands to keep the contents from falling out, so I slipped them off and opened it up. Inside was a stack of manilla file folders.

I carried them to my dining room table and slid the folders out. A little pink sticky note was affixed to the top folder. Scrawled across the note were the words: *Hope this helps. AJ.* Interesting. I knew what I would be doing for the next couple of hours.

The files contained case assignment logs overseen by Lieutenant Wiggins for the last eight months. There were a lot of them. A big part of a lieutenant's job is to supervise and coordinate squad personnel, which means keeping tabs on all the cases his detectives are working and assigning new cases as they come in. That entails keeping records of who is doing what so there's a good balance of workload distribution. Such reports are not easily accessible. I had no idea how Juarez had gotten hold of them, but I was glad he did.

I opened the folder on top and read through the first few pages looking at names of detectives, case numbers, and the status of each case. I quickly realized this task was going to be far more difficult than I had anticipated. Highlighters and colored pens would be needed, so I gathered the necessary supplies from my desk and organized everything as neatly as possible on the table before digging in.

After an hour of slogging through reports, my cell phone rang. The number wasn't familiar, but it wasn't blocked, so I answered it. "Hello," I said, glad to let my eyes take a break from the small type of the reports.

"Hello, is this, uh, is this Mr. Gray?" asked a man hesitantly.

"Yes, sir, it is. How can I help you?" My decorum regarding unknown callers had become more polite since Brenda started working for me. She insisted that I treat all of them as potential clients, which meant no snarky remarks or terse replies. At least not until I knew what they wanted.

"This is Lon up at Lon's Auto Body. You were in here the other day and said if I had any more information for you, I should call." He wheezed as he spoke, and I remembered the fat man from the shop. My brain shifted gears instantly, and he had my complete attention.

"Yes, of course. Have you remembered something?"

"Not exactly. One of my guys hasn't shown up since your visit. He called out sick twice, but he hasn't missed a shift in the five years he's been here. I don't know if this has anything to do with your business, but I thought you might want to look into it."

"Thank you," I said. "It might be important. Who is it?"

"Matt Heifers."

"You got an address for him?"

He did. I scribbled it on the blue sticky note from the file folder and stuck it in my pocket.

"Thanks. I'll look into it," I promised and hung up. I looked at the papers spread across the table and decided I'd come back to them. My gut told me there was something hinky about the whole thing with the art gallery. It was too easy, too convenient. The phone call was suspicious to begin with. How did someone know I was looking for the artifact in the first place? It wasn't exactly a matter of public record. Maybe it was an inside job. Maybe I'd already gotten close to the culprit without knowing it. Maybe the gallery thing was meant as a diversion. I was pretty certain now that what I'd found wasn't the real artifact. It was still out there somewhere, and I was determined to find it.

I needed to check on Heifers. Sooner rather than later. Wiggins wasn't going anywhere. I grabbed my coat and hat and ducked outside into the wind.

It was cold enough that I decided to drive. I headed west on Devon Avenue through Little India and took a left on McCormick, following the river south back into Albany Park. Heifers's address was a boxy little brick house on a side street just off Argyle. Half a dozen others just like it lined the street, but they all looked across to bulkier brick walk-ups four stories high. It was near a small park and I figured it wouldn't be long before the property taxes forced the smaller places to sell and more apartments would go up.

The house itself was in good repair. The sidewalk out front was cleared of snow. There was a small driveway, but no car was parked in it, so I swung the Buick in, wheels bouncing over the corner of the curb as I did so. Driving was still new to me, and I hadn't quite gotten a hang of all the little nuances yet.

I killed the engine and got out. Standing in the driveway for a minute, I attuned myself to the rhythms of the neighborhood. It was quiet except for the tick underneath the hood as the engine cooled. I guessed most everyone was at work or tucked away inside somewhere to avoid the cold.

After a couple of minutes, I went up the sidewalk and pulled open the screen door. I knocked. Twenty seconds later there was no answer. I rang the doorbell and waited another twenty seconds. Still nothing.

I walked around the house looking for a window to peer through or a back door. I found both. The window looked in on the kitchen. Tile floor beneath a small square Formica table and a stainless sink, lacking a pile of dishes, were all that I saw. The back door was next to the window. It was locked. Deciding the back of the house was safe enough from prying eyes, I withdrew my set of picks from my inside coat pocket and set to work. A minute later the door eased open and I stepped inside to the warm and cozy kitchen.

The first thing that struck me was how empty the house felt.

There are different kinds of empty feelings in a place. An apartment that has been vacated and had all the furniture removed as it waits for a new tenant has a different emptiness than a house whose elderly owner died six months ago and the family can't bring themselves to get rid of it. The first is an echo-y emptiness that buzzes with potential. The second is a deep, solemn emptiness that squeezes the heart.

The emptiness that greeted me here, however, was different still. It was the emptiness of a house that is usually filled with the laughter of children and business of parents in the few moments after their departure, as if the house is taking a deep breath after a long day before settling in for a well-deserved nap. It felt like I had just stepped in to the fresh silence after a flurry of activity. A clock on the wall ticked loudly as the seconds slipped by. Then there was a click and a low whump as the pilot light ignited the furnace somewhere in the basement below, then a steady hum as heated air forced its way through the ducts.

Across the kitchen was another doorway and what looked like a living area beyond. Afraid to disturb the silence, I stepped carefully across the black and white checkered floor to the living room. A small TV sat on an antique server along one wall and a muted brown English sofa opposite it. Between them was a picture window that looked over the front yard. Heavy blue curtains were currently pulled shut.

Another doorway led to a foyer by the front door and a hallway that, undoubtedly, extended back to a bedroom or two. I followed it and found them. The first had been turned into an office and was neatly kept. The second was the master bedroom. The bed was made, but the closet door stood open. I peeked in and saw jeans and t-shirts on hangers. Who hangs up their t-shirts?

Satisfied no one was in the house, I walked back to the kitchen and stood for another minute. I was about to leave when my phone rang. The number was unfamiliar, so I answered.

"Hello?" I said.

"Why are you in my house?" said the voice on the other end. No preamble, no pretense. It was Matt Heifers. I recognized his voice from the shop.

"I'm looking for you, Sherlock. Why aren't you here?"

"Because I'm out," he said sharply.

"Clearly. But you told your boss you were sick. He asked me to check up on you because you aren't the kind of guy that stays home with a sniffle. So if you aren't sick, what's going on?"

He didn't answer right away. He was thinking about his next statement. He was thinking of a way to get rid of me. I'd given him an opening. All he had to do was tell me another lie. I thought he'd go with being at the pharmacy. What I really wanted was for him to stay on the phone. He was close. Close enough he watched me enter his house. Which meant he could see the back door from his current location. I went back into the living room and slipped into the Skygge.

"Cut the crap detective," Heifers said, avoiding my attempt to catch him in a lie. "We both know why you're really looking for me. You think I stole something."

"Do I?"

A haze of purple light clung to the sofa. Purple. I hadn't seen that before. It must have been where he liked to sit. I let my gaze wander, looking for stronger signs of the strange energy residue. There was a faint trail leading out the back door.

"We heard Ronnie got pinched. She said you were asking all kinds of questions about stolen goods. Guess you weren't looking for a missing kid after all, huh?"

"Very good Matt. You're two for two. Get another

one right and I might want to hire you." I didn't even try to disguise the sarcasm. I stepped into the foyer, unlocked the front door, and went outside. I was sure Matt would be able to hear the change over the phone. After all, the wind was gusting and there was no way I could shield the mouthpiece completely.

"Very funny, asshole. I don't have what you're looking for."

"What am I looking for?"

"You'd know better than I would." His responses to all of my barbs and questions so far were deflections, not denials. That was interesting. It told me he was reluctant to flat out lie. I wondered how far I could push him.

"I guess that depends on if you took it or not," I said. I tracked around the side of the house and paused, scanning for signs of the purple energy again. I found it easily enough. It stood out from the other red and white currents I was used to.

"Just go away. I don't need this right now."

"Look, if you aren't the guy, then there's no reason we can't sit down like two grown men and have a civil conversation." I cut through two neighboring yards to stay out of sight as I followed the lights. They were leading me toward an apartment building the next block over. I figured Heifers's backyard would be visible from the fifth and sixth floors. Maybe he was up there watching. I ran some quick calculations in my head. If he had seen me break into his house from a neighbor's backyard, he would have had time to run to the closest vantage point before making the phone call. I picked up my pace. "But you are the guy, aren't you?"

He didn't respond.

"See, I'm a lot smarter than I look. And you, you're making all kinds of mistakes."

"I don't make mistakes," he said. Ah, there was a hint of arrogance coming through. Bingo.

"Maybe you don't make many or maybe no one picked up on them before. You are one hell of a thief. I still don't know how you pulled it off. You were damn near invisible. You were in the clear, right? But then I showed up at the shop and you got rattled. Maybe no one has ever gotten that close before and you panicked. You laid low. Called in sick. But you should have gone in. It seems you're too reliable and Lon missed you. But even that could have been explained away as coincidence."

"Bullshit," said Heifers.

I finally reached the apartment building. The main door stood ajar. A lot of residents wedged a piece of paper into the jamb to keep them unlocked when they went outside for a smoke and would forget to remove it. I pushed it open and paused, getting my bearings.

"Maybe," I said. "It's possible I'm way off the mark. Hell, it's not enough probable cause for a warrant, but hey, I don't need one. I'm not a cop. But then there's the other thing."

"What other thing?"

"Your name." The entry had a set of mailboxes and beyond them were stairs leading up. The purple trail was a bit thicker here, so I started climbing.

"My name?"

"Yeah. It's pretty clever, I'll give you that. At least you didn't use an alias of some big time thief like Bill Mason or Charlie Peace. That would have been too obvious. But anagrams are pretty common, too." This revelation was met with silence and I knew I had him.

My breath was coming hard now, and I moved the phone away so I wouldn't be mouth breathing in his ear. I was at the third landing. Each landing had a hallway lined with apartment doors and ended at a window. I figured Heifers was standing at one of the windows on the fifth or sixth floor.

"Know what your last mistake was?" I asked taking the stairs two at a time.

"I...I..." he stammered. He was flustered and didn't know what to say, but I needed to get him talking.

"Take a guess."

My head came above the last step to the fifth floor. I slowed, inching upward, and saw a figure silhouetted at the far end of the hallway, only thirty feet away. Purple energy seeped out of it and pooled on the floor at his feet.

I let the Skygge fade away and focused on moving

silently. Heifers faced the window, clearly watching for me. He had to know I was no longer in his house and was scanning the surrounding landscape.

Heifers let out a ragged breath. "I don't know detective, what?"

I waited until I was ten feet away before answering. "You shouldn't have called me."

He spun at the sound of my voice, jaw hanging open. The phone was still at his ear. "How…how?"

Heifers tensed up. His eyes were wide and darting around wildly. He was panicking. That wasn't good. His brain was gearing up for fight or flight or freeze. His posture, the set of his feet, the angle of his hips told me it wasn't going to be freeze. Which meant I had essentially just cornered a wild animal. Unless he went through the window, I was between him and the only exit.

Throwing the first punch is a good idea when a fight is inevitable or when the guy's got it coming. This wasn't one of those situations. I didn't want the guy going anywhere, but I also didn't want to put him down like the muscle head from the gallery, either. Heifers was a decent sized fella, and he had the fire, but he didn't strike me as having the same experience I did.

Finally, his eyes came back into focus and settled on me. He took a step forward and said, "I'm leaving."

I stuck my arm out and placed my palm flat on his chest. "Not yet. We need to talk."

That was enough to spark the flame in him. He knocked my hand away and lowered his shoulder, like he was going to bulldoze me out of the way. I didn't let him.

I set my feet, lowered my own shoulder and met him head on. He didn't bounce off or anything, but he wasn't getting by. He took a step back, then another. Then he charged. He tucked his head like a football player aiming for a hole in the defensive line.

Instead of meeting him head on this time, I sidestepped, grabbed his jacket as he went by and jerked hard, redirecting his momentum. He stumbled and crashed into the wall. He must have been disoriented by the collision because he sprang back up and threw a wild punch in the wrong direction. The force of his swing pulled him off balance and he tripped over his own feet. I saw what was about to happen and tried to grab him but didn't move fast enough.

Heifers was top heavy and once his center of gravity tipped beyond his hips, he couldn't recover. He fell. Not a big problem ordinarily. Unfortunately, he had reached the stairs and instead of landing on the carpeted floor of the hall, he toppled over the top step. After that, gravity was his worst enemy. He stuck his arm out to break his fall, which may have saved him from a broken neck, but it didn't do his arm any good. He bounced down three more steps before his head smacked the concrete landing and he slid to a halt.

I leapt down the stairs after him to make sure he was still breathing. He was, but he was out cold. His arm was at an awkward angle, most likely broken. He needed medical attention, that was for sure, but I didn't want to call 9-1-1. Not yet. I looked back down the hallway half expecting someone to open a door to see what was going on. Maybe they could help. Or maybe they'd call the cops. It didn't matter either way. Nobody stuck their head out.

Moving him would be tricky. If he had hurt his neck, it could make things a lot worse. I got my cell out and made a call.

"Hello?" said Stacy when she picked up the phone.

"Hey Stacy, it's Gray. I need a favor."

20

Heifers woke up before Stacy got there. He lay in the same spot where he came to rest on the landing. I hadn't touched him after making sure he was still alive.

First, he stirred, rolled a little. Then the pain hit him and he gasped, said a few choice expletives, and held his arm closely against his body.

I said nothing for the first minute, letting him get the pain under control. When I guessed it was as bearable as it was going to get, I said, "You really shouldn't move. You'll make it worse."

He glared at me but couldn't get any words through his clenched teeth.

"Someone's on the way," I said.

That sent a wave of panic through him and he tried to claw his way to a standing position. It didn't work.

I got up from my perch on the step below and got ready to catch him. "Calm down. Your arm is broke, at least. Probably a concussion. Maybe more. I've got a doctor on the way."

He gave me a sideways look, like he didn't trust me, but lowered himself back to floor. There was something strange about the way he was acting. Distrust was understandable, especially if he was the thief, which I was pretty sure he was, but he stayed right on the edge of panic. His response seemed to be an overreaction. There was something else going on. I had to figure it out but didn't want to risk spooking him again with too much talk. So, I just sat there.

Ten minutes later, Stacy walked up the steps carrying a medical bag in one hand.

"Hey," I said. "Thanks for coming."

Heifers had worked himself around so that he was propped up on the wall, still clutching his arm.

"What happened?" she asked as she stepped over to Heifers. He watched her warily.

"He fell down the stairs," I said.

She shot me a withering look, then turned her attention back to the patient.

"I'm just going to take a look at your arm," she told Heifers. It was a sweet, gentle voice. He said nothing; just continued to watch her like a wounded animal watched a circling coyote. She slipped a hand behind his shoulder. He flinched, cringing away from her.

"We need to get your coat off. Can you lean forward?" Once again, she placed her hand behind his shoulder to provide some support and helped him lean forward. He tried to shrug out of his coat, but a yelp of pain escaped his lips and he fell back against the wall.

"I can't," he rasped. "I think it's broken."

Stacy looked at me then and said, "We need to get him to a hospital."

"No!" Heifers said sharply. "No hospitals."

She arched an eyebrow at me in question. I shrugged.

"He needs an x-ray at the very least," Stacy said. "I can't treat him if I can't see the break."

"What about the clinic where you took me?" It wasn't technically a hospital.

She looked thoughtful for a moment. "Maybe."

"We could always commandeer a vet's office like they do in the movies."

She didn't laugh. She pulled a tiny flashlight out of her kit and turned back to Heifers. But I caught the corner of her mouth quirk up slightly as she did.

She flicked the light back and forth in front of Heifers's eyes and clucked her tongue. "Delayed pupil response. You probably have a concussion, too." After a moment's consideration, she continued. "Okay, let's take him to the clinic."

I stood up and Heifers looked back and forth between us, his fear mounting again. "Don't worry," I told him. "It's not a hospital. I'm sure we can keep this off the books." He was somewhat mollified by that.

"Your legs still work?" I asked.

He nodded. I grabbed him under his good arm and helped him to his feet. He kept the other arm clenched tightly to his chest and groaned at the exertion. Stacy went ahead of us as we all walked down the stairs.

Outside we had a short discussion about who's car to take. It was decided that we would take Stacy's because her parking permit would allow us into the garage at her building, giving us easy access to the elevator and, therefore, the clinic. I wanted to sit in the back with Heifers because I didn't trust him. Sitting close would also put me within easy reach to dissuade any shenanigans, but Stacy insisted that I drive so she could keep an eye on his condition and be ready if there were any complications. I grumbled a bit, but when I remembered how she handled herself against the mugger the other night, I let it go and climbed into the driver's seat.

It was a twenty-minute drive to Stacy's building. The first five minutes were spent in relative silence. My mind picking at the knot of actions and reactions of Heifers. What was he so scared of? Eventually, I decided to ask. I adjusted the rearview mirror so I could see him. "Okay, Mr. Heifers, it's time to talk. What's got you so spooked?"

He said nothing but watched me in the mirror.

"What am I missing? I know you're not afraid of the cops or being arrested, because as you said, I've got no proof of anything. None that would hold up in court anyway."

His eyes showed no sign of fear or denial. That told me I was correct on that point. I continued. "You could have gone about your business, denied everything, and walked away clean as a whistle. But you didn't. You panicked when I got close and made a whole bunch of mistakes. Which begs the question: why?"

He looked away then, maybe out of shame. I was two for two.

"There are only two reasons I can think of. First, the idea of any scrutiny at all from the authorities would be damning in some way. Maybe they'll turn up evidence of other crimes, other thefts that haven't been solved. Or maybe you've got another side hustle running that would be interrupted by an investigation, even one where you came out on top." I paused to watch his reaction. He still looked away, but there was a tiny smirk pulling at the corners of his mouth.

"Second, it has nothing to do with what can be proven. The thought of even being suspected of stealing the artifact terrifies you."

He looked back at the mirror and his eyes told me all I needed to know. I was right.

"Okay," I said and took a deep breath. "Why? What have I missed?"

Heifers looked at Stacy, who had a quizzical expression. She was starting to put the pieces together but hadn't quite caught up. He looked back at me. "You really don't know, do you?"

"Know what?"

"Who you're working for."

That caught me off guard. "I'm working for the museum."

His expression grew dark. "Not exactly. That artifact didn't belong to the museum."

"I know that. It was on loan from a wealthy donor."

"Is that what they told you?"

I stared at him in the mirror, unsure of where he was going with this.

"That piece belonged to a very dangerous man. If he thinks I had anything to do with taking it, I'm dead."

That explained a lot—well, it explained his behavior anyway. It also brought up a lot more questions. "Then why take it in the first place?" I asked.

"I never said I did. And if you tell anyone that I did, you might as well shoot me and dump me in the lake yourself."

Stacy looked horrified. "He's not going to tell anyone anything without proof. Right, Gray?"

It wasn't my job to prove he stole it. I was already ninety percent sure and every word he said increased that percentage. What I said was, "My job is to find the artifact. I'm not required to disclose how I found it or who helped me." I found his eyes in the mirror and made sure he was listening. "Understand what I'm saying?"

There was confusion in his eyes at first, but as he thought about my words, it was replaced with understanding, and maybe a bit of relief.

The car thunked over a speed bump as we pulled into the garage of Stacy's building. I maneuvered to a spot as close to the elevator as possible, and I hauled Heifers out of the back seat.

The elevator doors pinged when we arrived at the first floor, and we hurried through them as they slid open, making a beeline for the clinic. Stacy spoke briefly to the girl at the front desk, then ushered us back into the heart of the place. It turned out that the clinic had its own x-ray machine in a room at the back. We sat Heifers down on a table in the center of the room, and between the two of us, we were able to peel his coat off so Stacy could take a look at his arm. It was purple and swollen, but no bone protruded from the skin, which was good. After a brief examination, she placed a lead vest over his chest and told me to wait outside.

"No way," I told her. "I'm staying right here."

She huffed but grabbed another vest for me. I put it on and leaned against the wall. Stacy positioned Heifers's arm on the table and told him not to move, then stepped out of the room.

I watched him closely, deciding on what approach to take now. He was my only lead, and I was convinced he had stolen the artifact. "Okay Matt, let's cut to the chase. I know you stole the artifact from the museum. I have no idea how and I can't prove it, but I know."

He started to protest, but I cut him short. "Let me finish." I came away from the wall and took a half step closer. "The only thing you've told me that I actually believe is that things will go badly for you if anyone else finds out. Maybe very badly. Maybe you deserve it. Maybe you don't. My gut tells me you aren't a bad guy, but I need to know what's going on. And you need to tell me." There was a loud buzz as the x-ray machine took a picture.

Heifers considered for a moment before responding. "Tell me one thing first."

"What?"

"How did you find me?"

"I'm a detective. That's what I do."

He shook his head. "That's not what I mean. How did you find me in the apartment building? It shouldn't have been possible."

"Why?" I asked.

He shook his head again. "I've been around a long time. If I don't want to be found, I won't be. Except you did. Tell me how." Stacy came back in the exam room, repositioned Heifers's arm and left again.

I took a deep breath and thought about how to answer his question. The truth about my abilities still baffled me. Explaining it to someone else wouldn't be easy, but maybe it was time to give it a shot.

"All right," I said. "This might sound like a load of horseshit, but it's my best explanation." He raised his eyebrows and winced a little as his nose moved. I continued. "I see things most people can't. As far as I can tell, every living thing exudes an energy of some kind. Sometimes it has a very distinct signature. It lingers wherever a person is or was, leaving a trail just like Hansel and Gretel. Following yours was a piece of cake." There was another buzz, another picture taken, and Stacy came back in.

"Okay," she said. "I'll look at those in a minute. While we wait, let's see if we can't do something about that nose of yours. Come with me."

Heifers followed her, clutching his arm once more. He gave me strange look as he passed. I couldn't tell if he thought I was full of it, if I was nuts, or if it was something else. I fell in behind them as Stacy led us to a small exam room where she directed Heifers to take a seat. He did and she gathered some gauze, tape, and one of those metal strips they use to stabilize a broken nose.

"This is probably going to hurt," she said. "But try not to squirm too much."

He flinched as she prodded the bridge of his nose with her fingertips. After a few seconds she pulled her hands back and said, "The good news is the bone is still in place—no need to set it. I'm just going to tape it up." Which she did. When that was done, she told us to stay put and left the room again.

Heifers looked at me and nodded. "Okay," he said.

"What do you want to know?"

That caught me off guard. Did he actually believe my story? If so, why? I knew it was true, but still didn't completely believe it. Regardless, he was ready to talk, and I needed information, so I said, "Tell me about the artifact's owner. The wealthy donor—who is he?"

He shook his head. "He's one of the most powerful men in the city. Dangerous. Ruthless. Untouchable."

"What? Is he a politician or something?" I half smiled at my own joke. Heifers just looked at me steadily, seriously.

"Worse. The politicians might as well be his puppets. He can pull strings just about anywhere."

My mind flashed to the board in my office—the one with all the cops' faces taped to it. Could this guy be the one with his fingers in the department investigations, telling his crony which ones to let slide? I had no idea. "What's his name?"

He shook his head again. "I don't know. Some call him Mr. Monday, but I'm pretty sure that's not his real name."

"What do you know about him?"

"Not much. Enough to know I never want to meet him. You live in my world long enough and you hear things. Rumors, whispers. People he targets don't last long so it's best to stay off his radar."

Stacy came back in with an ice pack, a bottle of

ibuprofen, and the x-ray films. She told Heifers to hold the first on his swollen nose, sat the second on the counter, and hung the films on a light board.

"What's special about the artifact?"

He shrugged one shoulder. "Hell, if I know."

"There's got to be some reason it was stolen," I said, trying to avoid another accusation. I didn't want him to shut down now that I had him talking.

"Maybe, but I really don't know."

"Okay, let's deal with that arm now," Stacy interrupted. We both looked at her. "It's a stable fracture so you won't need more than a cast for about six weeks." I nodded and Heifers looked relieved but irritated at the same time.

Stacy retrieved the supplies necessary for making the cast from a cabinet and set to work preparing it.

After a moment I continued the interrogation. "Do you know where the artifact is?"

"I might," he said cryptically.

"What does that mean?"

"I know who has it," he finally admitted. "And I know where you can find them. Whether the artifact is there, I don't know."

"Now we're getting somewhere," I told him. Stacy listened to the exchange intently. "You tell me where to find them and if it checks out, I'll leave your name out of my report. Like I said, I'm not obligated to tell them how I find the piece." That was mostly for Stacy's benefit, but it was true, and if Heifers was telling the truth about the owner, I didn't see the need for collateral damage.

"There's a group that calls themselves the Brotherhood of the Rose," said Heifers. "They work in secret to undermine Monday's influence. They're the ones that wanted the artifact. I don't know why, but..." He stopped himself. He was conflicted, and I could guess why. If this Mr. Monday character was as bad as he claimed, it was only natural that he would want to help a group working against him.

"Where can I find them?" I asked.

"Monastery of the Holy Cross," he said.

I stared at him. "Seriously?"

"As far as I know."

"A monastery?"

"Yeah."

Great. That certainly changed things. I couldn't exactly waltz into a monastery and ask them to hand over stolen property. Well, I could. But it wouldn't go over very well. I'd have to ask nicely.

On the other hand, if they were being housed by an order of monks, maybe I should just let them keep the damned thing. If they'd had it stolen, it had to be for a good reason. But that thought twisted my shorts a little too much. I needed to know more about what I was dealing with.

"All right. What can else can you tell me about these people?"

"Not much," Heifers admitted. "They're very secretive. I don't know any names. No faces."

Stacy had wrapped his arm with white gauze by this point and now submerged a bright blue roll of specialized mesh in a bucket of water before wrapping it around the gauze.

"Then how do you know where I'll find them?"

Heifers didn't answer at once. He started, paused, searched for the right words but came up with nothing, then started over again. "I had a meeting with one of them, but he kept his face hidden. His voice, though—it's distinct. We've spoken several times since and I get the feeling he doesn't leave the monastery."

If Heifers couldn't tell me anything else, I'd have to go myself. I sighed, then said, "Okay. One more question." I paused for dramatic effect. "How did you get past the cameras?"

21

Heifers closed his eyes and lowered his head. He was tired of fighting me, of the constant denial. "It's just a thing I can do," he said with defeat in his voice.

"What do you mean?"

"I can't explain it. I wouldn't even know where to begin."

"Try," I said, my patience wearing thin.

"Better if I show you. Wait until she's done," he said indicating Stacy who was applying a final layer to the cast.

After smoothing down the loose end she said, "It needs to dry. It will take about fifteen minutes. Keep that ice pack on your nose."

He moved the ice pack back to his face from where he'd let it slip during our conversation and winced at the pressure.

I looked at Stacy and said, "Is there anywhere to get a cup of coffee around here?"

"We probably have some in the front. I'll go check."

I nodded.

She opened the door and stepped out. I followed her with a sharp look at Heifers.

"Thanks," I said. "I owe you."

She gave me an appraising look. "You bet your ass

you do." Then she moved down the corridor to the front of the suite.

A thought popped into my head, so I stepped back into the exam room.

Heifers wasn't there.

I whipped my head around, looking for another exit. There wasn't one. How the hell had he gotten past me?

I went still and slipped into the Skygge. The tell-tale purple energy Heifers exuded swirled around the room. It took a few seconds to hone in on its flow. When I did, I turned my head slowly to the side to follow it. Heifers sat in a chair next to the door. I came out of the Skygge and stared at him. He hadn't been there just a few seconds ago. Had he? I felt like I was losing it.

He sat there watching me intently. I shook my head to clear it. I must be getting tired.

"Tell me about the voice," I said. "You mentioned it was distinct. How so?"

Heifers thought for a moment before answering. "It's funny. The impression it left on me was old leather. I don't know if that makes sense, but I think it's a good de-scription. His voice sounded like an old leather-bound book might sound being opened for the first time in years."

The comparison made sense to me. The other night I'd spoken to someone that sounded like old parchment. Old leather and parchment. I wondered if the two might actually be describing the same voice. It was worth considering.

Heifers sat up in the chair, leaned forward, and fixed me with an intent gaze. "Look, these are the good guys. Whatever they want with that artifact, you should let them have it. Let this thing go. It's not too late."

Now I was shaking my head. "I can't do that. The Field Museum is a highly reputable organization. They hired me to find and recover an object that was taken from them. There is no evidence that the object was not rightfully in their possession to begin with, so I will find it if I can. I'll keep your name out of it because you cooperated, but that's as far as I'll go. Unless I turn up credible information about illicit provenance, my course is set."

I crossed my arms to show there would be no further discussion on that point. Heifers watched me for a moment more, then sighed and leaned back in the chair. Stacy came back with three cups of coffee a few minutes later. She set two on the counter and handed me the other.

"Thanks," I said.

She nodded, then checked to see how the cast was drying. When she was satisfied with its progress, she carefully handed Heifers the third steaming cup of coffee. He stuck his nose in it and inhaled deeply.

"Thank you," he said.

"You're welcome," she replied.

We sat in an awkward silence, sipping our coffee for several long minutes. Stacy looked at me. I looked at her. We both looked at Heifers.

Finally, Stacy spoke up. "So, show us."

"What?" Heifers and I both said at the same time.

"Earlier, Gray asked how you got passed the cameras and you said it would be better if you showed us. So, show us."

I was glad she brought it up. It was something I was dying to know, but I felt as though I had pushed Heifers as far as I could and wasn't going to get anything else out of him. But Stacy had just done him a kindness by bringing him coffee and her demeanor was, shall we say, softer than mine.

"Okay," he said, setting his coffee down. "All you need to do is turn around and count to five."

Stacy gave me a quizzical expression and arched an eyebrow. I didn't know what he was up to, and I still didn't trust him, so I hesitated. Other than the chair he sat in, there weren't any heavy objects he could hit us with. No sharp ones either. With only one good arm, the chair wouldn't be much of a danger.

I shrugged and turned my back. Stacy followed suit. I counted to five and we both turned back.

Heifers was gone. Again.

The door was still closed, and I hadn't heard it

open. "What the hell?" I breathed. It was just like when I stepped into the hall. Stacy stood mouth agape.

I turned around again and studied the room. There didn't seem to be anywhere to hide, and he'd disappeared so fast, it seemed like he had simply vanished. But that wasn't possible. Was it?

I turned a slow three-sixty, looking carefully for any sign of Heifers or a clue to how he'd disappeared but saw nothing. Stacy looked at me and asked, "Where did he go?"

"I'm right here," said Heifers's voice from behind us. We both spun around, and there he was, sitting in plain sight on the table in the center of the room.

Now it was my turn to stare in bewilderment. I couldn't for the life of me figure out what had just happened.

Stacy's jaw worked as she searched for words. "How...where...what just happened?" she sputtered.

"It's pretty simple," he said. "I just go where you aren't looking."

I thought about that. It made sense in a ridiculously simplistic way, but it didn't explain anything. "Yeah, but how?"

"Like I said. It's a thing I can do. I just know where people are looking, or will look, and go somewhere else."

"That's impossible," shot Stacy. "You can't predict where someone is going to look."

"I can," replied Heifers. "I can't explain how, it's just something I know. Instinct, I guess. Though I imagine there's more to it than that."

I took a step backward and slid into the chair Heifers had occupied a moment before. There was definitely more to it. Theoretically, what Heifers said was sound. If you knew exactly what a person's line of sight would be, it should be relatively easy to remain out of it. The problem arose when you were dealing with more than one person. Fields of vision overlap frequently and remaining out of all of them would be virtually impossible.

"Can you do that in a crowd?" I asked.

"More or less," he said. "I can't always avoid being seen, so then it's a matter of being noticed. And that's not hard to avoid at all."

That was true. The human brain can only process so much information at once. It only remembers what it pays attention to, and a crowd of people throws way more information at a brain than it can handle, so we don't actually see all the individual people in it, just the ones that draw our attention in some way.

Still, the ability to do what he just did was extraordinary. But so was being able to see the energy of life flowing around you. Or talking to someone in their dreams. Or accelerated healing.

Stacy must have been thinking along the same

lines because her gaze turned to me and her eyes narrowed. I could see the gears turning. Her eyes widened as she came to some conclusion and looked back at Heifers. "I need to draw some blood," she said.

***

The car ride back to Heifers's house was primarily filled with Stacy asking lots of questions. Most were directed at him, but occasionally she'd shoot one at me. Matt answered some of them but avoided a direct answer most of the time. She wanted to know everything related to his ability. How long had he been able to do it? Was it something he learned by practicing or did it feel innate? Was it hereditary? Were there any ill side-effects? That sort of thing.

I remained quiet unless specifically asked something. I had a million questions of my own and a pretty outlandish theory, but this wasn't the time or place to get into it. When Stacy dropped us off, she was still buzzing with excitement, and I got the feeling she was going to put in a long night at the lab running DNA. Heifers thanked her for the help, she made me promise to call the next day, and then we stood shivering in his driveway until she disappeared around a corner.

I turned to Heifers. Heifers turned to me. We stared at each other. I could tell he wanted me gone, but I wasn't finished with him yet. The wind was picking up, the sun was sinking fast toward the horizon, and I wanted nothing more than to go inside. His body language told me there was no way I was getting an invitation inside—much less a hot cup of joe.

"Right then," I began as a chill shot down my back. "What are you?"

"Pardon?" he asked.

"What. Are. You?" I exaggerated each word and waved my arms in the air before pointing at him. He didn't think it was funny. In a normal tone I said, "Clearly, you aren't a normal person. I've had a crash course in the strange and anomalous this week, and I want to know where you fit."

"Strange and anomalous? Me? I'm just a mechanic with an unusual set of skills. Maybe you're the strange and anomalous one. So, what are you?"

"I'm a Shadow Walker."

His expression changed. The annoyance and petulance fell away.

"Damn," he said. He turned and walked up the driveway toward the house. Over his shoulder he called, "You better come in then."

22

I sat down in one of the four chairs surrounding the small yellow table in the center of the kitchen and watched Heifers wander from cabinet to cabinet, pulling out one thing at time with his one working arm. First, he retrieved a strange looking pot, filled it with water, and set it on the stove. Next was a tin of coffee, then a grinder. The grinder thunked down on the table in front of me and he spooned some beans into it. Then he told me to grind. It was a hand crank grinder. I couldn't tell if it was an antique or something new designed for hipsters. Heifers got down one small cup, then another and set them on the table too. Then came a container of sugar and a clean spoon.

Heifers didn't speak while he worked, but there was something different about him. All the tension he'd been carrying since I first found him was gone. He moved with a fluidity born of comfort and years of practiced ritual. There was something different in his eyes, too. Earlier they had shown with the heat of brash youth. Now a deeper, older wisdom smoldered there. This was not the cornered, frightened man from before.

When he had arranged the accoutrements to his satisfaction, he took the grinder from me and checked the grounds in a drawer at the bottom, rubbing them between thumb and forefinger to feel their coarseness. Apparently satisfied, he took them to the stove and spooned them into the strange little pot. He tapped the spoon on the edge of the pot, then spooned in an equal amount of sugar. After that he turned the knob on the stove and adjusted the flame to its lowest setting.

By this point I recognized what he was making: Greek coffee. I'd had it a few times and it was good. Though I'd never seen how it was made.

He came over, pulled out the chair opposite me, and slid into it. "Shadow Walker," he said. "That explains a lot."

I didn't respond. He was gearing up to tell me something, and I didn't want to interrupt or change what he was about to say. If my admission had opened a door, it was important that he walk through it first.

"I've only met one other and that was a very long time ago." The way he said it made me wonder exactly how long. He opened his mouth to continue, then closed it. He gave me an appraising look. "You're the one that took out Red Dread, aren't you?"

He was referring to the group of vampires I'd tangled with two months ago. They called themselves Red Dread and used Craigslist to gather reports of homeless people by posting about red dreadlocks. I killed two of them, but they had a crew of well-armed soldiers that had been eliminated by someone else. That particular someone had responded to a call for assistance I put out, so ultimately the responsibility was mine.

I nodded. "Mostly."

He nodded back. "Glad you did. They were a bad bunch." He got back up and checked on the coffee. It was starting to simmer. "To answer your question, I don't know what I am exactly. I've never known of anyone like me. At least, no one with my abilities. I guess I'm one of a kind, even if I don't know what kind that is."

"But you are Shadow Born, right?"

"Shadow Born?" He laughed. "Who the hell have you been talking to? I haven't heard that phrase in ages." He picked the pot up off the stove and let the foam forming on top settle before putting it down again. "But yes, I suppose I am."

"What's your real name?" I asked.

He shrugged. "Matt is the only name I've used for a long time," he said still watching the bubbling liquid.

"How long?"

He looked at me. His brows pinched together in confusion. "How much do you know about us 'Shadow Born'?"

"Not much," I admitted.

He grunted and turned back to the coffee. He lifted it from the stove again and brought it to the table where he poured it into the two cups already placed there. When he finished, he put the pot in the sink and sat back down, gesturing to the cup in front of me. "Try it," he said.

I took a sip. It was rich and creamy with just the right amount of sweet. It may have been the best damned coffee I'd ever had. It must have been written all over my face because he smiled and picked up his own cup. He sipped, slurping loudly.

"I have your word that you'll not breathe a whisper of my involvement in this to anyone?"

"You have my word," I told him.

He let out a deep breath, as if he'd been holding it for a very long time. "In that case, I'm going to help you. I'm guessing you haven't known what you are for very long."

I shook my head.

"This city belongs to Monday. It has for a long time. Little happens here that he doesn't know of or control. Those of us who acquiesce, do his bidding, or remain out of sight are allowed to go about our business. Those who make waves or openly defy him are silenced quickly.

"A few months ago, rumors surfaced about a group that was taking steps to undermine his authority. They were whispered from ear to ear in confidence or secrecy. But the nature of such secrets belie themselves, and I think that may have been by design. The Brotherhood dared not reach out to anyone directly for fear of drawing Monday's attention too soon. Instead they left a trail of breadcrumbs only the truly rebellious would follow. Since then, their influence has grown quickly. A war is coming, I think. Sides are being chosen, alliances formed.

"At first, I was excited by the prospect as long as I could contribute in secret. But now, I think a war would do far more harm than good. Monday is too powerful. He would annihilate the Brotherhood and their allies completely, securing his position for decades. And now you, a Shadow Walker, come along. You could change everything."

"What?" I asked. If what he said was true, how could I possibly change anything?

"Right," he said. "You probably have no idea what it means to be a Shadow Walker."

"One foot in your world, one foot in mine." At least that was how Willy had put it.

"Yes," agreed Heifers with a nod, "but more than that. Shadow Walkers are peacekeepers, maintaining the balance of powers when they are needed most."

"Peacekeepers..." I let the thought trail off. I hadn't been a peacekeeper in a long time. When I was a cop, I wasn't known for keeping the peace. More for causing problems for the bad guys. "I'm not sure about that. If it involves knocking somebody off their high horse, then maybe."

Heifers smiled over his cup. "Maybe. But more importantly, you might be able to stop this war before it starts."

I thought about that for a while. Preventing turf wars was something I'd done a few times back in the day. Rival gangs would get into it over some perceived slight to their ego or, more likely, an upstart would present a legitimate business threat. Either way, our job was to step in and keep innocent people from getting hurt. Often, that involved cracking down on the new guy to maintain the status quo. It was easier for us to remove the threat safely and legally than to let the incumbent gang take care of it. Is that what I needed to do here?

"Do you think the Brotherhood still has the artifact?" I asked.

He nodded.

"Then that's where I start." He started to protest, but I cut him off. "You don't pick a fight with the school bully unless you're sure you can finish it. You hand over your lunch money until you've got the right color belt."

That must have made sense because he didn't argue the point. I finished my coffee and swirled the dregs around the bottom of the cup, watching the patterns they made as they settled.

"I knew somebody who could read your future doing that," Heifers said.

He was watching me intently. Maybe he thought I could do it, too. I shrugged. "The future is what we make it," I said as I flipped the cup upside down onto the saucer with a sharp clack. "And I say we make it better."

After a long minute, Heifers nodded once. "How can I help?"

23

First thing the next morning, I turned on my home computer, a dinosaur in terms of Moore's law, which ran a ten-year-old operating system. But it was sufficient for what I needed. Gaming wasn't my thing, and I did most of my work at the office. I could have used my phone, but I prefer doing research with a bigger screen when I can. Plus, my fat fingers have a hard time typing on a phone keyboard. While waiting for the thing to boot up, I poured myself a bowl of Golden Grahams, one of my dietary weaknesses, and scooped out a can of tuna for Willy.

By that point, the computer was ready to go, so I did a quick search for "The Monastery of the Holy Cross". They had a pretty impressive website; it gave me a rundown of the daily life of a resident, an overview of services open to the public, and a description of the attached bed and breakfast the monks ran. I was primarily interested in the worship schedule so I could figure out the best time to drop by. Vespers was the last service of the day at 5:30. After that, the brothers spent the evening in study or silent contemplation. That would work. It gave me plenty of time to make preparations.

Locating the artifact within the walls of the monastery was going to be tricky. It was a big place. The statue could be hidden anywhere. I doubted I would have the time needed to scour the church. Odds were I was going to be occupied with the Brotherhood. What I needed was help.

A plan had come to me the night before while I slept. It may have had a little outside help in its formation, but it was a good plan. So I called on the people I knew I could trust. There weren't many in my life at the moment, but I hoped to change that soon. Of course, all the planning and preparation in the world can amount to less than a hill of beans when the shit hits the fan. They have a saying in the military that no plan survives first contact. Essentially, it means no one can accurately predict every possible outcome of a given situation and that the ability to improvise and deviate from the plan is necessary for success. However, you still have to have a plan to deviate from.

I made a few more phone calls, synchronized swatches, and made that plan. Without knowing exactly what I was walking into, I was a little nervous about a few pieces, but it was the best I could come up with.

Once everything was set, I turned my attention back to the investigation of Lieutenant Wiggins. I grabbed the highlighters and made myself comfortable at the kitchen table, but something was wrong. The early morning light was usually good in here, but today it seemed dimmer than usual. I got back up and pulled the blinds open over the kitchen sink. Steely gray clouds blanketed the sky and flurries drifted down to settle on the window sill where they stayed. It was cold and it looked like we were in for a good snow. The sight gave me a shiver, so I padded down the hallway and kicked the thermostat up a degree, made a pot of coffee, and flicked on the lights before finally settling in to get some work done.

Two hours later I had combed through every single case assignment log, color-coded each case based on status, and noted anytime a detective's caseload increased significantly. I doubt my organizational plan would have made much sense to anyone else, but after the first pass, I was able to narrow my focus to only those whose status remained open or were marked as inactive, with a priority on the inactive ones. Open cases were still being investigated. Inactive ones had either been open for too long with limited progress or the initial report hadn't turned up enough evidence to warrant spending further time and resources on it.

The truth is that many, many crimes go unsolved due to lack of evidence. They get marked as inactive until the statute of limitations runs out. I had the proof in my hands. There were a lot of cases highlighted red, the color I'd chosen for inactive. It was unlikely many of them were being manipulated. Even though Wiggins was in charge of his detectives, the Captain would be keeping tabs on the reports as well. The easiest way to keep attention off a case was to keep it from becoming a case in the first place. The only way to do that was for the patrol officer that got the call to not write it up. Since there was no way to know which officer would respond to a call, it would be impossible to guarantee results that way. Once a report was filed, it would be difficult to squash the investigation without drawing attention. Difficult, but not impossible. The key would be to do it so infrequently they got lost among all the legitimate inactive cases. If Wiggins was killing cases, I'd have to look extra hard. This was going to be like finding a needle in a needle stack.

By noon I had a handful of cases that I wanted to take a closer look at. Several were missing persons, a couple of armed robberies, and one arson. There wasn't a lot of detail in the assignment logs, and deciding which warranted further scrutiny wasn't easy. Most of them were of the sort that typically became inactive. There were two ways of getting the case files. I could go the traditional route, filling out the proper forms, mailing them in, and waiting a week or two for a response, or I could cut some corners and call Jack.

Jack Larsen, my former partner, had been my go-to guy since I became a private investigator. He knew me better than anyone else and we trusted each other completely. He had no qualms about sending me reports or any other information he could legally get his hands on, thus saving me a lot of time and red tape.

Because Jack didn't work in the same district as Wiggins, he wouldn't be able to get copies of the original files, but he could send me anything that had been put into the computer. This meant I wouldn't be privy to anything as detailed as detective notes, but I should be able to get the official reports. I picked up the phone and dialed his number.

"Gray, how are you?" he asked when he finally answered. "It's been a minute."

We talked for a bit as I brought him up to speed on my recovery. He didn't seem quite as amazed as everyone else at how quickly I got back on my feet, but he probably figured I was spinning the truth to further the machismo reputation most cops worked hard to maintain.

"I need a favor," I finally told him.

"Do my best."

"Can you send me a few files?"

"Sure," he said. There was no hesitation. It was purely a routine request on my end. "You got the case numbers?

I did, so I read them off.

"Got it," he said. "That's a lot of files. What are you working on?"

"A longshot," I told him. "I'm looking to see if there's a connection between them. No idea what it might be at this point, but I have to look. Know what I mean?"

"Yeah, okay," he said. "I'll pull them together for

you and send you an email."

"Thanks. I owe you."

"I know. Hell, at this point, you probably should just take over my mortgage payment." He laughed. I chuckled along, knowing that he was probably right. He'd done a lot more for me over the years than I'd done for him.

"Hey, if you ever need a consultant on anything, you let me know." Occasionally, the Department would hire outside consultants when they needed expertise on a subject but didn't want to give up jurisdiction to the FBI or some other agency. My offer wasn't simply a token gesture because such things typically cost a lot of money.

"You got it," Jack said, and we hung up.

I got up to put my coffee cup in the sink and glanced out the window. It was snowing in earnest, tiny little flakes falling in a continuous sheet, and didn't look like it would let up anytime soon.

Silent as the falling snow, Willy leaped onto the counter and looked out the window as well. I looked at him, but he didn't acknowledge my presence. Once he gauged the severity of the weather, he flicked an ear and dropped back to the floor, padding back down the hallway and out of view.

My thoughts turned back to Wiggins. Until I got the files from Jack, I couldn't look at what he'd done. Instead I thought about his motive. When dealing with corruption, it almost always came back to money.

Staring out at the falling snow, I thought about my last case, about how flagrantly the night manager had spent his ill-gotten gains. I doubted Wiggins would do the same. It was even possible that he never saw any actual money at all. Perhaps he benefited in other ways. Maybe he was provided access to property held in another's name, like a trust. Maybe he was named beneficiary of some insurance policy and would only cash out at a pre-determined point in the future. If something like this were the case, it would be hard to find, and harder still to prove.

But that wouldn't stop me from trying.

The first step was to try personal property records in Clark County. Unfortunately, I couldn't find anything under Wiggins's name. He must have rented. The DMV records were a bust too. I already knew Wiggins had a tiny digital footprint, but I wondered about his wife, if he had one. Maybe she was bragging about the new clothes or jewelry he'd bought her or the vacations they'd taken. It was worth a look.

Turned out the Wiggins' were divorced and had been for five years. Marsha Wiggins had a marginally more active social media life than her husband, but not by much. Her last post was from August; a picture of her son with a caption about how proud she was of him, but how much she would miss him. The photo was of a kid in his late teens in a football uniform kneeling on the field. It appeared to be one of those fancy senior portraits people spend too much money on that only the parents care enough about to frame and hang on the wall. The other recipients dump them in a desk drawer and forget about them. There was nothing suspicious about it. But it got me thinking.

I dug deeper.

Back in August, Don, Jr. left home to study Engineering at Duke University. He left a far larger and deeper footprint on the web than his parents. There were a number of pictures involving various brands of adult beverages that would shame any parent. The amount of data he proffered to the general public was unbelievable. No employer in their right mind would give this kid a job when he graduated if he didn't clean up his act soon. It told a story of a kid who didn't take his education seriously and cared more for his social conquests than in building a career. Considering that Duke cost more in tuition than most other schools in the country, I had to wonder what was going on. Unless he was on a scholarship, which was unlikely, the student loans would be impossible to pay off with the future he was going to have.

The thing was, I couldn't find the typical signs of a scholarship. There was no mention of him playing on any team. An outstanding high school academic record wouldn't guarantee a full ride for four years, and the life he was currently leading left little doubt as to what his GPA would look like at semester's end. Maybe he'd gotten a scholarship to start with, but it wouldn't last. It wasn't impossible that he'd had good intentions at the beginning, but the freedom that accompanies college was too much of a temptation and he'd strayed from the straight and narrow. In fact, it happened to a lot of kids. But those were usually the ones with rich parents who paid for everything. Kids who took out loans, got scholarships, or otherwise paid their own way tended to take things more seriously. One thing was sure: the Wiggins' didn't make the kind of money to pay for Duke out of pocket.

It wasn't much to go on, but it gave me some ideas.

24

As the afternoon got late, I made several more phone calls.

When it was time, I suited up for the weather: sweater, wool topcoat, gloves, and a furry bomber hat that would keep me toasty on the coldest Chicago night. All the layers made it difficult to wear a shoulder holster, so instead I strapped on an ankle holster made for the Walther PPK I carried. An ankle holster was designed for concealment of a weapon when other methods for carrying weren't feasible. They didn't provide quick or easy access to a weapon, but they did provide access which was better than no weapon at all. At least it was in my opinion.

After a final check that I had everything I needed, I scooped Willy up in one arm, tucked him under my coat, and strode into the storm. He didn't stay there long. He squirmed and wriggled until finally slipping from my grasp and landing gingerly on the wooden landing. He looked up at me and sneezed, then led the way down the stairs.

An inch of new snow covered the ground like a bride's veil at her second wedding. It was pretty, but the grit and grime of daily life still lay beneath. It also derailed my plan immediately. Most Chicago drivers would have ignored such minor conditions, but I didn't think my skills were on par with an inch of slippery slush yet. Even a small fender bender was more than I wanted to deal with tonight. I hoped this wasn't a sign of things to come.

"Sorry Willy," I muttered as I altered course and headed for the train instead of the Buick. "Change of plan." It would take a whole lot longer to get there, but my best bet was to take the Red Line down to Chinatown and cab it the rest of the way to the monastery. It was already four o'clock, and the trip would take at least an hour, maybe more. I'd be cutting it close.

Willy prowled along the sidewalk ahead of me, wandering this way and that, sniffing at whatever piqued his interest. As we approached the station, I scooped him up again, taking him back under my coat.

"Cats aren't allowed on the train," I whispered. "Sit tight and bear with me."

It was unlikely anyone would say something if I did let Willy roam free on the train, but I didn't want to risk it. He was part of my plan.

As the train jostled along the tracks heading for downtown, I thought about the events of the last few days. As always, I ground down the narrative into a list of facts, stripping away all speculation and keeping only what I knew for sure. A valuable artifact had been stolen from the Field Museum by a thief of extraordinary ability. He had been hired to steal it by a secretive group he called The Brotherhood of the Rose. This group believed the theft would somehow undermine the power and influence of its owner, who I knew to be a benefactor of the museum, but whose identity was kept anonymous. Though Heifers claimed this mysterious individual was a nefarious force that ruled the city without mercy, I had no evidence to support it. It was clear that Heifers thoroughly believed it, but the certitude of belief is not equivalent with proof of truth. The Field Museum has an immaculate reputation, and they were my client. Until I had more information about the nature of the artifact or its owner, ethics demanded that it be returned if possible.

I had also been informed by an anonymous source of the location of the artifact, which I successfully retrieved and turned over to Dr. Halgrave. Tests were being run which would determine the authenticity of the figurine, but I was certain it would prove to be a fake. My theory was that the tip had come from the Brotherhood in an effort to throw me off. Maybe the artifact would be long gone by the time the test results had come back. If that was the case, I wasn't going to let them get away with it.

As I thought about Dr. Halgrave, I couldn't ignore the overwhelming sensation of attraction I'd felt in her presence nor the odd color of the energy I saw emanating from her. Most of the energy I'd seen had been blue and red, save for Heifers's tell-tale purple residue. I wondered what the significance of her signature was but had no way of knowing. It did, however, leave me suspicious. Could it be that she, too, was one of the Shadow Born?

Doubt gnawed at my convictions. Hopefully, this evening's trek would provide me with the answers I sought.

The train pulled into the Cermak station and I got off, keeping Willy bundled up inside my coat. It was difficult to keep him concealed amidst all the people getting on and off the train, but I managed. The snow was coming down in earnest, falling straight down, undisturbed by even the slightest breeze. The light was fading fast, the sky dulling to the flat gray that precedes true twilight on a winter evening. I hustled down the stairs from the elevated platform and out onto the street. Cabs were plentiful as the rush hour was just beginning, so I flagged one down and gave him the address of my destination.

Willy jabbed me with his claws and wriggled out from under my coat to sit on the seat beside me. The cabbie didn't pay any attention, so I didn't say anything. We pulled away from the curb and took an immediate left onto Archer, one of the diagonal streets that cut across the neat Chicago grid, heading southwest away from the loop toward Bridgeport. The streets were slushy. I felt the cab skid once, but the driver handled the conditions like a pro, which I guess he was.

Ten minutes later, we pulled to a stop at the corner of Aberdeen and West 31st, right in front of the

Monastery of the Holy Cross. I paid the cabbie and crawled out of the car. Willy hopped out behind me, took a look around, and sauntered into the deepening dusk. Checking my watch, I saw that it was five minutes after five. Vespers would be starting in ten minutes. I hurried around the corner, looking for the main entrance to the church proper.

The Monastery of the Holy Cross is comprised of three separate buildings, but the most visible is the church itself whose bell tower and steeple rises almost a hundred feet above the streets, towering over the other buildings in the neighborhood. It isn't as grand as other cathedrals and temples in the city, but its familiar neo-gothic brick architecture is certainly striking.

I pulled open the door and stepped inside. The first thing to hit me was the warmth. The temperature outside had plummeted as the sun dipped below the horizon, and the heat now washing over me was quite welcome. The second thing that hit me was the sheer beauty of the sanctuary.

Vaulted ceilings opened up in a soaring expanse and were supported by basilica-style arching pillars. Ahead, an aisle flanked by rows of pews, led to a bank of honey-colored choir stalls, in which stood eight robed monks. Beyond the monastic choir sat a massive white, marble altar on a three-tiered dais. Light spilled from seven stained-glass windows set into the curved walls high above the altar, though whether they were lit from within or without, I couldn't tell.

A wave of sound washed over me then. A chorus of voices rich in timbre chanted in rhythm with a perfection honed by years of practice. The prayer swept through me like nothing I'd ever felt and left a profound stillness in its wake. In hushed silence, I moved to the back row of pews. There were a handful of visitors, not as many as I'd expected, but enough to dispel the emptiness. The serenity I now felt left little room for anything else, and the purpose for my visit evaporated as I sat entranced. My gaze wandered around the magnificent nave, taking it all in, until they lit on the back of three familiar figures. On the side opposite where I now sat, four pews ahead, sat my little family.

Nancy, Alice, and Maggie were here as promised. They had agreed to be my eyes this evening. The monastery was a big place and the artifact could be anywhere. Though I doubted it would be kept in plain sight, that was often the best place to keep something hidden because most people would look at it but never see it, so it wouldn't hurt to have them on the lookout.

At first, I wasn't sure I wanted them here. This Brotherhood of the Rose was an unknown factor in my little mystery, and unknowns were dangerous. I certainly didn't want to risk Nancy and the girls coming to any harm, but the more I thought about it, the surer I felt that this was the safest place for them. The Benedictine monks that inhabited this place were a pious, peaceful people who devoted themselves to serving God and man through hard work and a life of prayer. I couldn't imagine them hosting anyone with violent intent. Plus, as long as they kept a low profile, followed the rules and simply admired the sights, they wouldn't draw any attention. I, on the other hand, planned to take a more direct approach.

I refocused on the service, listening to the harmonious voices offering their sacrifice to the Lord. Long past are the days of slaughtered goats and burnt offerings, the Christian Church having replaced such early rites because the greatest sacrifice had already been made by Christ himself. Now, sacrifices were more personal—those of time, money, and creature comforts in an attempt to draw nearer to God.

I abandoned my own religion years ago, chafing at the strict expectations and judgments passed by the elderly congregation. Many of my generation followed a similar path, leaving their respective churches after high school because the institutions were too conservative and stifling. It wasn't so much about a loss of faith or belief in God as it was a struggle with the people who tried to shape us.

Despite my past feelings, this place seemed more holy than the church of my youth. As I allowed myself to sink deeper into the hypnotic chant, I realized with amazement that it was not the place that felt holy, but the people. The solemnity of their prayer, the completeness of their dedication to their worship was something I'd never experienced. It astounded and refreshed me at once. All the doubts I had squashed earlier about this job came bubbling back to the surface. I felt with certainty that these were good people. Would they knowingly harbor those conspiring to bring strife to the city while believing it was for the greater good? It didn't seem likely, but then again, neither did the existence of vampires and Dreamwalkers.

The troubling thoughts gnawed at me for the remainder of the service, obstructing complete immersion in the experience. I told myself I would return when this job ended and, without a cloud of doubt hanging over me, truly enjoy what was offered here.

Forty minutes later, the Prior was offering a prayer of dismissal. People slowly, solemnly trickled out of the sanctuary. I watched as Nancy approached the Prior with the girls and had a brief conversation. She was asking if there was a chance that she and the girls could take a tour of the monastery. I couldn't hear what was being said, but I knew the content anyway.

The Prior gestured to another brother who strode over quickly. Introductions were made and permission was granted. The newcomer ushered the ladies through a door that led out of the sanctuary. I let out a deep breath and nodded. If there was anything to see on the tour, Nancy would text me. I'd sent her a picture of the statue recovered from the art gallery, so she knew what she was looking for.

I remained seated in the pew as the nave continued to empty, admiring the craftsmanship on display. Depicting scenes ranging from the Virgin Mary to pronouncements by the Pope, and even John's "Vision of the Apocalypse", the stained-glass windows were a marvel to behold. The intricate detail of the hand-carved confessionals must have taken hundreds of hours to complete.

Eventually, I stood and began making a slow circuit of the cathedral to inspect each piece of art more closely. Various sculptures and paintings dotted the periphery. I took them all in, wondering if any of it would look familiar. As the last of the worshippers left, I was aware that the Prior watched me with curiosity, though he made no attempt to disturb my perusal.

Finally, after making a complete loop, I decided it was time to introduce myself. I turned back to where the Prior had stood unobtrusively but was surprised to find myself completely alone. It seemed too good to be true, but I didn't waste the opportunity. I had no idea what the layout of the monastery was, but there were doors set on either side of the altar which I assumed would lead to areas not on the tour Nancy was currently taking. I strode quickly across the marble floor toward the right-side door and was almost to it when the one on the left opened and a monk stepped through. It wasn't the Prior, but he still didn't look surprised to see me. He was dressed in a simple black habit with close-cropped dark hair. I half expected him to ignore me and go about cleaning the pews or something, but instead he made a beeline for me. I watched him cross in front of the altar and step close.

"May I help you?" he asked in a small voice.

"Maybe," I said a bit reluctantly. "I've been told that you may be hosting some guests that I'd like to speak with."

"I'm sorry, the Bed and Breakfast is currently vacant," he replied.

"I don't think these particular guests would be using it anyway."

He cocked his head. "I see." He paused and looked at me for a long moment. "Please wait here while I inquire." Then he turned and left through the door he'd entered.

By this point, I didn't think it would be wise to go snooping around so I took a seat on the first pew and waited. I didn't have to wait long. Within five minutes, the door opened, and the same monk reentered. He didn't rush, but there seemed to be a bit more purpose to his movements and drew closer. "You may follow me," he said in his hushed tone.

He led me through a different door that opened into a hallway. On the left, it passed a broad stairway leading to an upper level. I could see several other doors farther down. The passage to the right was blocked by another door, but I didn't get to see what was on the other side because he led me down the hall and through a swinging door to a kitchen. It wasn't what I had expected. There were granite countertops and modern appliances, but heat roiled off an antique wood-stove in waves. A wall of windows made up the opposite wall and overlooked a courtyard outside. The snow was still falling and I briefly imagined how comforting it would be to sit at the solid oak butcher's block table positioned at its center with a cup of hot chocolate in hand.

We moved through the kitchen, past a large stack of firewood, and down a small staircase. At the bottom was another door that opened onto the courtyard. I shivered as we stepped outside but noticed that the monk paid the cold no heed.

The snow was now several inches deep and it crunched lightly underfoot as we padded diagonally across the open space toward a large brick coach house. As we drew near, I saw there was no visible entrance and wondered where, exactly, we were going. The mystery was solved as we turned into a narrow gangway separating the church from the coach house. We followed it until the front of the coach house came into view where several cement steps ascended to a set of double doors.

Here the brother halted, turned to me, and said, "They are waiting for you inside. I trust you can find your way from here."

I nodded, unsure of what to say, and the black-clad monk shuffled past me and disappeared back down the gangway. When he was gone, I retrieved my phone and checked for any messages. There was one from Nancy. A single word: "Nothing."

At the top of the steps, I pressed the latch and the doors opened with a squeal. Inside, a wide curving staircase led upward and an archway on the right revealed a room full of shelves. Several lamps on end tables glowed, filling the room with a soft, warm light. I stepped through the archway and studied the tableaux before me.

Shelves lined every wall, save for a few windows interspersed between. Hundreds of books stood in neat rows. I couldn't see any titles in the dim light, but their covers reflected myriad hues of red, black, brown, blue, white, and purple. A library. The books held my attention for only a second, however, because it was drawn quickly to the three people also occupying the room.

Two men stood on either side of a yellow armchair. The one closest to the shelves was shorter than me, maybe five-eight, and wore a tunic similar to the ones the monks wore, but his was colored a deep red, almost magenta, where the brothers' tunics were black. His face was hidden in the shadows of the cowl.

The man on the other side of the chair played a stark contrast, cutting an imposing form. He was tall and broad shouldered, bigger even than me. He was dressed in jeans and a sweatshirt drawn tightly over a muscled chest. His hair was buzz cut, like they do in the army. His hard eyes stared at me from a chiseled face that once would have been handsome, but was now marred by an ugly scar running diagonally across his cheek and puckered the corner of his top lip.

Between them, in the yellow armchair, sat a third man. He was old, but I couldn't tell how old. Sixties. Seventies, maybe. His features were sharp and narrow, reminding me of a hawk, but his skin was loose with age, drooping around his eyes and mouth, softening the hard edges. He wore a charcoal suit with wide, peaked lapels, a style from the 80's. A square of cloth the same color of the other man's tunic peeked out of the breast pocket. He watched me carefully from under his drooping lids.

I stood in the center of the room. Floorboards squeaked underfoot as I eyed each man and let my gaze settle on the one in the chair. I said nothing, just stood there and waited. A minute of silence turned into two. No one moved. No one glanced away. From the corner of my eye, I thought I saw a flash of movement, but it could have been a shadow from a passing car.

Usually, I am a patient man, comfortable with my

own thoughts, and perfectly happy to wait in silence, but something about these men said they had far more time than I did and had no intention of speaking first. After all, I had come to them.

Finally, I cleared my throat and spoke. "You are the Brotherhood of the Rose, I assume?" That got a reaction, though a small one. A tiny arched eyebrow and flick of the eyes from Scarface to the Suit.

"The color scheme kind of gives it away," I added.

"You seem to know more than we expected," said the man in the suit. The voice was dry and crackly, like old parchment. I recognized the voice. He had told me about the artifact being at the art gallery.

"You," I said.

"Yes," he said.

Missing puzzle pieces fell into place.

"Then you know why I'm here."

He nodded before taking a wheezing breath and said, "You will be disappointed, I am afraid."

"Maybe," I replied. "Maybe not. I'm sure you have the artifact hidden away and are confident I won't find it. And you're probably right. But I have no intention of looking for it."

"Really? Then what is your intention?" the old man asked.

"Don't get me wrong. I fully intend on walking out of here with it. But I'm pretty sure you're going to give it to me freely."

His eyebrows rose and the big man next to him shifted his weight. "Is that so?"

It was my turn to nod.

"And why, exactly, do you think that?"

"It's the only reasonable outcome to the current situation." I took the cell phone out of my pocket and held it up. "All the evidence points to the artifact being in your possession. I can easily make a phone call and have the police here in a matter of minutes."

"And tell them what?" he scoffed. "That the brothers at the Monastery of the Holy Cross are harboring thieves. You think they will swoop down on us and tear the place apart looking for it on your word alone? Whatever evidence you believe you have is far from enough to get a warrant."

"Right. You're right," I admitted. Threatening to call the police had been an empty threat to begin with. I knew it, and now I knew he knew it, too. "Option two would be to call my contact at the museum and tell her that it's here."

He said nothing, but I could tell I had his attention now, so I continued. "As far as I know, that would accomplish nothing. The Field Museum could pass on my findings to the authorities, but as you've pointed out, that isn't enough to even get a warrant. It would, however, satisfy my contract and I could move on to the next case." I lowered the tone of my voice. "But rumor has it, the owner of the artifact might have a different take on things. That's pure conjecture, of course, because I have even less evidence to support that idea than the other."

"That would be...unwise," said the man in the suit.

"Option three," I said before he could say more. "You hand the *real* artifact over to me, I return it to the museum and conveniently forget where I found it." It was the same offer I made to Heifers. If they thought this Monday character was as big a threat as Heifers did, there might be a chance they'd take me up on it.

The old man narrowed his eyes until they were bare slits. He was considering my words. That was a good sign. I waited for a response, knowing not to push it. Finally, he shook his head.

"I'm sorry, Mr. Gray, that is not an option. While I believe your offer is sincere, I cannot allow the artifact to return to its 'owner.' It is too dangerous."

"Dangerous? It's a statue."

He shook his head again. "It is far more than that, I'm afraid."

I had no idea what he was talking about, so I said, "I have no idea what you're talking about."

He seemed to sink back into the chair, about to launch into an explanation. I held up my hand, palm out. "Don't tell me this thing has secret powers or something," I said before he could begin.

"Actually, yes."

I groaned. Loudly. The two other men in the room shot glances at each other. "Great," I said. "This just keeps getting better. I mean, why not? If vampires are real, cats can talk to you in your dreams, and I'm a Shadow Walker, why can't ancient artifacts wield mysterious powers? It makes perfect sense." I might have said more than I intended. The big guy's eyes were wide with surprise and he looked ready to fight. The old man sat forward in the chair, eyes bright with interest.

"So what the hell does it do? Shoot lasers out its ass?" I asked before anyone could question my outburst.

The old man sat back in his chair again, clearly offended by my sarcasm. "No, Mr. Gray. Nothing so vulgar. The powers we are talking about are far more subtle. We believe this artifact allows whoever possesses it to exert influence over its creator."

"How?"

"We don't know."

"Let me get this straight. You stole an artifact from the Field Museum because you believe it will let you control its creator and you won't give it back because it's too dangerous? Bullshit. I'm making the call."

His eyes flicked to the man on his left, the smaller one. "No," he said. "You aren't."

Before I could react, the little man in the tunic was holding my phone in his hand. I had the impression that he'd moved across the floor and taken it from me before I could blink, but I don't think I actually saw anything. One second I was holding it, the next I wasn't.

I stared slack-jawed at him. His hood had come down so I could see his face. He was dark-skinned, with a shock of jet-black hair that looked like it hadn't been combed in a week. He looked lazily at my phone in a way that reminded me of a cat watching a moth while he dozed in the sun. He dropped the phone to the floor and brought his heel down on it with lightning speed. It crunched and a piece of black plastic shot across the floor and went under a shelf.

"How..." I began. I wanted to be angry, but astonishment was in the way. This guy was fast, maybe faster than Eli, the vampire I'd tangled with two months ago, had been. He didn't look like a vampire, but what did I know? I let my sight slide into the Skygge. Immediately, I could tell something was up. The ribbons of light I was used to seeing glide their way along the ground were acting strange. They were swirling around all three men like snakes wrapping around prey. I hadn't seen anything like it. Maybe they could somehow tap into the energies like I could.

I narrowed my eyes and looked toward Mr. Suit. "You're starting to piss me off," I told him. Anger had finally shoved its way past astonishment.

He gave an imperceptible shrug. "The danger is in

letting such a valuable tool slip through our fingers," he said as if the last ten seconds hadn't happened. "The one that calls itself Monday has far too much power over the people of this city. We have an opportunity to deal a significant blow against him, and I will not let it pass because of your arrogant stubbornness."

Did he just call Monday an it? This was turning into a very strange conversation. "If he's such a threat, why have I never heard of him? Who is this guy?"

He sighed. "Sit down, Mr. Gray. It's time for a story." He gestured to a high-backed wooden chair I hadn't noticed before. I was still miffed about the phone, but if he wanted to talk, that meant I still needed to listen, and I might still be able to convince him. I sat down heavily in the chair and crossed my arms over my chest.

"As you surmised, we are the Brotherhood of the Rose." He gestured to the other two. "Or at least, we are a part of it. There are others, of course, but we are representatives, if you will. Our job is simple: to ferret out and remove abominations before the Lord. Monday is one of them. He has amassed wealth and power for the sole purpose of exerting his will on the world. He is manipulative, merciless, corrupt, and ambitious. We are here to remove him from power."

"That's a pretty dramatic accusation. And very broad in nature. What, specifically, has he done that is so awful?"

Suit stared at me intently. "He created the mon-sters that killed your friend."

25

I blinked a few times. His words hit me like a punch in the gut.

"What?" I said.

"That's right, Mr. Gray. Monday created those monsters and turned them loose on the world. His very existence is a corruption of nature, a perversion that must be stopped at all costs."

I said nothing as his words sank in, dropping my eyes to the floor. If what he said was true, I should think really hard about my next move. I should find out all I could about this Monday character and, maybe, go after him myself. The problem was, I didn't know if it was true. All I had were the suspicions of a thief and those who hired him. It was hardly convincing.

After a moment, he continued. "Let me present option four."

I looked up.

"Join us. Your skills would be a valuable addition to our cause. Of course, you would also be working to bring down the one ultimately responsible for your friend's death. It is no coincidence that you found us. I believe it is God's Will that brought you here."

I shook my head. "You want me to join you in taking down some evil force that I've never heard of until today? The only evidence that he's done anything wrong is your word. And that doesn't hold much water for me. You stole a valuable artifact from a reputable institution, then in an attempt to delay or derail my investigation, you lied to me about its whereabouts. Just a second ago, your crony stole my phone and smashed it to bits."

I stood up and glared at him. "You're a common criminal as far as I'm concerned." The two men at his side shifted their weight, preparing to act if I made a move. I didn't. "And the fact that you hide behind the walls of this holy place and 'God's Will' makes you a hypocrite."

The old man's pale face flushed with anger, but his voice was calm when he spoke. "We are the Brotherhood of the Rose. To remove a thorn, it may be necessary to suffer a prick of the finger. Perhaps even to draw blood. What we do is necessary. We do as God commands."

"And he who fights with monsters might take care lest he thereby become a monster," I retorted. It was a quote by Nietzsche that had haunted me for years. Given my past, I was walking the line of hypocrisy myself. I was no longer on the force because of my inability to follow the rules. That, and my tendency to beat the snot out of bad guys. It might be that I had more in common with the Brotherhood than I was willing to admit. But being lied to pissed me off and right now I didn't feel like a kindred spirit. "Tell you what. How about we go back to option three and you hand the artifact over—the real one—and we'll call it even?"

"No," he said flatly.

Damn. This wasn't going the way I'd hoped. Fortunately, this was Plan B and had been a long shot to begin with. The whole conversation was meant to be a distraction anyway. Hopefully, Plan A was going a whole lot better.

Just then, I saw a shadow appear at the base of the wall behind the old guy, and Willy's disfigured face poked out from under the chair. We made eye contact, his whiskers twitched, and he disappeared again.

I shook my head once more. "I was hoping to save everyone a lot of fuss, but you've made your position clear. I'm leaving now, but whatever happens, know you had the chance to prevent it." I took a few steps back, not wanting to turn my back on them yet. They made no move to stop me, but just as I reached the archway, the old man spoke again.

"We are at war," the papery voice said again. "Either you are with us or you're against us. If you walk away now, I will assume you will make contact with Monday's representatives. That cannot be allowed to happen, Mr. Gray."

"Is that a threat?" I asked, meeting his eyes.

"This is hallowed ground, Mr. Gray. We would not defile it with violence," he said. His meaning was clear, though. Once I left the monastery, all bets were off. "Make your choice, detective."

I held his eyes a second longer, then stepped around the wall and burst through the door into the snowy night.

Thoughts raced through my head. I was in a bit of a pickle. The car I'd arrived in was long gone, and without a phone I couldn't get an Uber. Nor could I call anyone else for help. Because of the location, a cab wouldn't be convenient either. As long as I didn't leave, I was safe, but that was no comfort. I had no intention of throwing in with these guys and didn't want to stick around so they could watch me. I doubted I could outrun them considering how fast the guy in the robes could move. But maybe I could keep ahead of the others.

The back door to the kitchen was open and I dashed through, locking it behind me, thinking it might buy me a couple of seconds. I retraced my steps through the building into the sanctuary and out the front door. Once back outside, I paused to look up and down the street, hoping a cab would be passing by at just the right time. No luck.

The closest train was a long way away. But there was a bus on 31st Street. If I could find one before the Brotherhood caught up to me, I might have a chance. I ran west. If a bus was coming, I'd meet it head-on instead of running away from it.

I made it three blocks. The air filling my lungs was so cold that it burned, and I had to stop to catch my breath. Looking over my shoulder, I saw no sign of pursuit, and I began to think I'd been wrong. Maybe I was safe. Maybe no one was coming for me after all. The thought stuck with me right up until the short fella in the robes stepped onto the sidewalk in front of me.

"Really," I said. "We're gonna do this here? What about witnesses?"

The little guy shook his head but said nothing. Glancing around quickly, I realized he had nothing to worry about. The rush hour was over, and the snow-covered roads were empty of traffic. I looked back, but the little man was gone.

A sharp pain bloomed in my kidney and I whirled. He stood behind me, fists clenched, feet set in a fighting stance I was unfamiliar with. Things were about to go south for me quickly.

I'm a brawler with a long reach which gives me an advantage in most fights. Someone with speed and agility, however, can counter my tactics easily, and I'd already seen how fast this guy was. But I still had a trick up my sleeve. In the half-second before he struck again, I slipped into the Skygge and reached for the red lights. In a heartbeat, they were coursing through me. Time slowed and as the little man darted forward, I batted his outstretched hand away. He jumped back and looked at me with wide eyes.

"That's right, short stuff. I'm not making this easy."

Speed, strength, and anger pulsated through me. "And you broke my phone. That makes this personal."

I stepped in. If I could get my hands on him, I could end this quickly. But he jumped away again.

Fine. I could wait him out. Maybe. I struggled to keep the anger in check. If it took over, I'd make a mistake. We circled each other warily. With his speed advantage suddenly gone, my reach gave me the edge again and he knew it. My focus was completely on him, looking for an opening.

Which is why the next attack took me by surprise. A large man hit me from the side, tackling me, and we both went down to the sidewalk. Big arms wrapped around me, pinning my own to my sides. It was the little guy's buddy—the one in the sweatshirt. He squeezed and it felt like a python had gotten hold of me, one of the big suckers that eat alligators in Florida. I flexed and felt his grip give a little, but he clamped down again, threatening to force all the air out my lungs. If he did that, I was finished.

I kicked with my legs, trying to wrap them around his for leverage. I was in my element now. He might have the upper hand at the moment, but I'd been a wrestler in high school, and I knew how to deal with this.

Feeling the attacker's hot breath on my neck, I knew his head was close and vulnerable. I snapped my head up to the side hard, trying to put my ear to my shoulder. He was in the way, and the side of my skull smacked him in the face. The blow wasn't as forceful as if he'd been behind me, but it had the desired effect. His grip slackened momentarily and I twisted.

Now we faced each other, and I was able to slide my arms up into a double under hook position. I tucked my chin, burying my face in his shoulder and clamped down. The tables were turned, and I was taking control of the grapple. While I squeezed, I threw my legs over his and brought my knees up to pin his hips.

Something popped—one of his ribs—and he grunted in pain. He let go and I redoubled my effort, hoping to make him blackout. Instead, he clubbed me in the temple with his fist. It was a vicious blow, causing my vision to swim and my strength to ebb. I let go and rolled away, instinctively reaching for tendrils of blue energy. Immediately, the haze lifted and I got to my feet.

Now I faced two warriors. One with blinding speed, the other incredible strength. Fighting two men at once can be daunting, but in most street fights the lone guy usually has an advantage because the other two will get in each other's way and present lots of opportunities to counter. These were not your average Joes. They were clearly well trained and would coordinate their attacks with deadly efficiency. I didn't like my odds.

The pistol at my ankle would be a game changer, and only now did I realize how stupid I'd been not to take it out earlier. These guys wouldn't give me the time to draw it. They'd be on me like white on rice before I got my pant leg pulled up.

Speedy darted in, throwing one lightning fast jab after another. It took all my skill and hand-to-hand training to fend off the attacks. Beefcake stepped to the side, flanking me.

He launched a kick aimed at my knee. He wasn't nearly as fast as the other guy, so to my heightened senses, it was like slow-motion. But there was tremendous power behind that kick and if it connected, I'd go down. All I could do was turn my body as I deflected another jab and crouch so the blow connected with the side of my thigh.

The kick landed and for a second, I thought he'd snapped my femur, but I didn't go down. It hurt like hell, though, and my toes started to tingle. I backpedaled, trying to put a little distance between us and come up with a plan of attack. If I didn't figure something out, this might be my last fight ever.

The sidewalk was slick with snow and ice and my foot slipped. It was all they needed. They were on me before I could recover, and any thought of an offense evaporated instantly. A punch caught me on the jaw, and though it was glancing, it rocked my head to the side. I slipped again. Speedy took the opportunity to dance in and hit me with a knuckle punch in the shoulder socket and I felt my arm go limp.

I reached out mentally for more of the blue lights, but I could tell it would take too long to do any good. The fight was almost over, and I had lost. I didn't know if they would beat me to death here or haul me off to some secret warehouse and finish the job. Either way, there wasn't much I could do about it now.

And then something unexpected happened. Speedy convulsed and crumpled to the ground like he'd been hit from behind. I glanced up but saw no one. Beefcake looked around too, wondering what had happened to his buddy.

It was the opening I needed, and I wasn't about to waste it. Anger surged through me and I exploded up and forward, swinging a wild haymaker with my good arm. It connected with his jaw in a meaty thud and spun him around. I followed it with a kick to his knee, like he tried to do with me, but I didn't miss. His leg buckled and he fell to the sidewalk.

I knelt down and pulled the Walther from the holster at my ankle, then stood up and pointed the gun at him. A red haze clouded my vision. He deserved to die. My finger tightened on the trigger.

And a figure materialized out of the darkness.

"Don't," said a familiar voice.

I swung the gun toward the new threat and felt my anger falter. Standing in front of me was Matt Heifers.

"Let it go," he said.

I pointed the gun back at the man groaning at my feet. "He's still a threat."

"Don't become the monster."

I looked back at Heifers. Had he heard what I told the old man? I looked at the Skygge and realized the red ribbons of energy were still flowing into me. I let go of them and the red haze faded. I took my finger off the trigger but didn't lower the weapon. The big guy was getting his senses back and trying to get to his feet.

"Stay down," I told him.

He looked up at me and his eyes filled with fire. He was going to come at me again, I knew. I couldn't let that happen. I readjusted my grip on the pistol and brought it down hard against the side of his head. He flopped back to the ground and lay there unmoving.

I knelt down and checked his pulse. He was still alive, and it didn't look like I'd cracked his skull. He'd have a concussion for sure and one hell of a headache when he woke up, but he was out of it for now. As for Speedy, he was still out cold. Whatever Heifers had done was effective.

"Car?" I asked him.

"Around the block."

"Let's go, then." I said and started walking. "Looks like I owe you," I huffed, watching my breath create little clouds of fog that trailed behind.

He shrugged. "Best not to keep track."

"You get it?"

He nodded and withdrew an object the size of my forearm from his coat. The artifact was still warm to the touch and I wondered if that had to do with Heifer's body heat or something else. I clutched it tightly as we slid into Matt's car and drove away.

"Hard part's over," I said as we slid into a space by the curb a block away from my apartment.

"You're sure about this?"

"Yeah. You can handle it, right?"

"Piece of cake," he said.

"Good. I'll be in touch." I climbed out and watched him pull away.

26

My phone rang early the next morning. It was Dr. Halgrave. She wasn't happy. She informed me, in a bitter tone, that the test results had come back, and the statue recovered at the gallery was a fake.

"I know," I told her. "I found the real one last night. I'll bring it by this morning."

"What? How?" Her mood turned on a dime.

"I'll explain when I get there."

Two hours later, I handed her what I was sure was the real thing.

"Where did you find it?"

"Long story. Let's just say I tracked down the guy who gave me the tip about the gallery. It's better if you don't know all the details."

She nodded and ran her fingers over the statue. There was something odd in her expression, something that hinted at concern—apprehension maybe. I couldn't put my finger on it. "Do you think this one could be a fake, too?" she asked.

"Maybe. But I don't think so. You'll do the tests?" She nodded. "Let me know about the results?"

"Of course."

I turned to leave, then stopped and turned back. "Do you think I could take the copy?"

She narrowed her eyes. "Why?"

"I don't know," I lied. "Be nice to have a trophy for this one. Something to put on the mantelpiece."

She considered it for a moment and agreed. "I suppose we could arrange that."

After signing a few papers, I was out the door, false idol in hand. All I had to do now was wait.

***

Since I hate the idleness that comes with waiting, and I figured it would be a couple of days before I heard anything from Halgrave, I went back to the other case. Gathering everything I had on Wiggins, I laid it all out on my kitchen table and went through it again. I thought I had the motive but didn't have any hard evidence that he'd killed the cases.

Jack had sent me the files I requested. I printed them off and started looking for a connection between them: names of suspects, witnesses, anything that would link them together. Unfortunately, I came up with nothing. The complete case files might shed more light on the subject, but I didn't have them and doubted I'd ever get my hands on them. The only other thing I could do was confront Wiggins personally. I thought about how best to approach him and decided to wait. Christmas Eve was only a few days away, and someone like Wiggins would probably be sitting at home with a liquor bottle close at hand. If that were the case, it might be the best time to get something out of him.

I cleaned up the mess, called Stacy, and offered to buy her dinner.

We met that night at The Village, Chicago's oldest Italian restaurant. The chicken Vesuvio is fantastic. Our conversation started innocently over an obscure brand of Malbec that the waiter recommended. I don't know much about wine, but it was good.

Soon it turned to Heifers and what she'd seen and overheard the other night. She was near to bursting with questions. I shied away from the details because I didn't want her to think I was totally nuts, but I didn't lie to her either.

"I want you to trust me," I said. "But I can't tell you everything. There are aspects of this case that I still don't completely understand. Maybe when I've got a better handle on things, I can tell you about them. Can you be okay with that?"

She looked at me for a long time, sipping her wine. "I can respect that," she said. "Sometimes I forget how impatient I can get when I want to know something."

"I understand. I have the same problem, too."

From there the conversation turned to other things. I told her about my family, about why I hated my name. She told me about her dreams and ambitions. It was nice. Really, really nice. I had been worried about her reaction, but now I felt like this budding relationship had potential and holding certain things back wouldn't damage that. For once, I was hopeful about what the future held.

Two days later, Dr. Halgrave called back. The new artifact was the real thing and she was over the moon. The owner had been informed and it would be moved to a more secure location the following day. She said the check was in the mail and she'd be happy to pass my name along with a glowing reference.

I thanked her and immediately called Heifers. "It's a go," I told him. "And you're on a clock. It's being moved tomorrow morning."

"Roger that," he said.

Later that day, we met up at the Jarvis Bird Sanctuary just north of Belmont Harbor. The Sanctuary is a quiet, secluded spot surrounded by lots of trees. This time of year, it was empty of people and there wasn't a surveillance camera for blocks.

I was sitting on an elevated viewing platform when Heifers arrived. He sat down next to me but said nothing. After a minute, the birds came out of hiding and flitted among the branches around us.

"Everything go ok?" I asked.

In response, he slid something wrapped in an oil-cloth onto my lap.

"Any chance you were spotted?"

He looked at me with a raised eyebrow.

"Right."

"What are you going to do with it?" he asked.

"For now, I'll put it somewhere safe. After that, I'm not sure. I've got some research to do."

"Keep me in the loop?" he asked.

"Yeah. I owe you that much."

We sat in silence for a long while watching the birds. Finally, he stood to leave.

"Matt," I said before he did. He looked at me. "Thank you."

He nodded and walked off down the trail, disappearing from view.

I sat for another ten minutes before making the hike back to the Buick. From there, I drove to my storage unit. I tucked the ancient artifact—the real one that Heifers had just stolen from the museum again and replaced with the fake Halgrave had given me—into the old green footlocker that had belonged to my father.

27

When Christmas Eve finally arrived, I packed all the neatly wrapped packages into the Buick's trunk and tossed a duffel bag with a change of clothes into the back seat. I would end up at Nancy's later that night so I could be there in the morning for the girls. The first Christmas without their dad would be hard. Nancy thought it would help if I was there.

The first stop was the United Church of Christ on Damen. The Christmas pageant was at six-thirty followed by a candlelight service. Despite her broken wrist and cast, Maggie was ready for her starring role. She had a costume that incorporated the cast rather than simply trying to hide it. I could feel the whole sanctuary buzzing with energy as I slid into the pew with Nancy and Alice. It affected me, too. I hadn't felt this nervous about anything else I'd done over the last week.

When the pageant finally started, a hush fell over the crowd as the narrator began. I thought about that night in the monastery. These two places were similar in the sense of reverence filling them by those who worshipped, but there was also an excitement here that I hadn't felt there. Even now, I couldn't help but wonder about the Brotherhood of the Rose. I may have beaten them, but I was sure I hadn't seen the last of them.

My thoughts were interrupted when Maggie appeared. She might have been a tiny figure at the front of the sanctuary, but when she spoke, her voice filled the room. "Do not be afraid!" she boomed. "For behold, I bring you good tidings of great joy..."

I didn't hear anything else. I had slipped into the Skygge and what I saw drove everything else from my mind. A flood of white lights swirled around Maggie like an immense vortex. It grew bigger as I watched, the air around her glowing. Fear seized me as I thought about my own struggle with the lights. I wanted to jump up, to protect her somehow, but I was frozen in place. She didn't seem to be aware of what was happening, though, and as she reached the last line, "Glory to God in the highest, and on earth peace, good will toward men," the vortex exploded, breaking apart and throwing tendrils of light out into the congregation. I looked around, fearful of what I'd find. All I saw were smiling faces radiating joy and warmth.

Well, that was something.

When the pageant was over, Maggie ran back to her mother beaming with pride. "Did you see me? Could you hear me?" she asked.

"Yes, you were absolutely wonderful!" Nancy said.

The pastor stepped forward and began to heap praise onto the children and the adults who had helped put everything together. As he did, I whispered to Nancy that I'd see her at the house later, gave Maggie a hug, and slipped quietly out the back.

There was one more stop to make.

***

Wiggins lived in a high-rise apartment building on the Near South Side. I found a parking spot and went up an elevator to the eleventh floor where I followed signs down a maze of hallways until I came to the right door. I knocked twice and waited for a response.

Forty seconds later, the door opened a crack and a nasally voice said, "Who is it?"

"Lieutenant Wiggins?" I asked.

"Yeah, what do you want?"

"I'm sorry to bother you this evening. My name is Gray. I'm a private investigator and I'd like to ask you some questions about a case I'm working on."

"For Christ's sake," he grumbled. "It's Christmas Eve. Can't this wait?"

"No, I'm sorry. It will only take a few minutes."

"Can I see some ID?"

I held up my private investigators license and driver's license. He grumbled some more, but I heard the chain rattle on the other side and the door opened.

"Come on in. But make this quick, will ya."

He had on a pair of drawstring sweats cinched beneath a round belly that spilled out from under a slightly yellowed wife-beater. I could smell the alcohol oozing from his pores. He led me into the small apartment and

272

gestured to a worn leather sofa. I didn't sit.

He harrumphed and flopped down into a recliner, then reached for a tumbler filled with amber liquid on a small folding table next to it. At least he wasn't drinking from the bottle.

"What's this about?" he asked before taking a sip.

I stepped up and stood directly in front of him. "It's about you, Wiggins." I'd considered playing nice, thinking an aggressive confrontation would make him clam up, but the few seconds I'd known him told me he'd cave under the right pressure. "Specifically, it's about the cases you've been killing."

He sputtered. "I don't know what you're talking about."

"Yeah, you do. The McCarthy case, the Pershing Warehouse break-in, the meth lab at McKinley Park. You were the supervising officer on those cases. All of them got shuffled to the bottom of the pile and the detectives assigned higher-priority cases. They could have been solved if you let them. But you didn't want that to happen."

"How dare you!" He tried to stand, but I jabbed my finger into his forehead before he could and held him in his seat. He could have knocked my hand away or kicked me, but he didn't. He was drunk and rattled, so I kept the momentum going.

"I'm not finished," I said, venom coloring my voice.

"I've got a stack of files that have sat in drawers for months collecting dust and I know why. Someone's paying you off to make sure those crimes never make it to court. It's a whole lot easier to keep things quiet if they never get that far."

"That's bullshit!" he stammered. "Look at this place. You think I'd be living here if I was on the take?"

"Oh yeah, your financials are clean alright. But you never see a nickel of the money anyway. It's all going to your boy down at Duke."

The color drained from his face and he swallowed hard. "I..."

"Save it," I said. "I've got more than enough evidence to turn over to IA, but..." I let the unfinished sentence hang there.

He sagged back into his chair and I dropped my hand. "What do you want?" he asked with a sigh.

"A name. Who are you taking the orders from?"

He shook his head.

"You talk and they'll kill you, right?"

He nodded.

"Well, I guess you're in a tight spot, then. Give me a name and I forget we ever had this conversation. And maybe I get to them before they find out you talked. Otherwise I walk out that door and straight to IA. Then your little deal gets shut down. All those cases get a second look and whoever is paying Donny's tuition gets a wrench thrown in their operation. Think you'll survive that?"

Wiggins glanced at the glass of whiskey beside him. I stepped back and nodded. He picked up the glass and took a long swig.

Then he threw it at my head.

I saw it coming long before the glass left his hand. I dodged it easily, but he sprang out of the chair and swung wildly. I leaned the other way, felt the wind from his fist as it passed by my ear, then threw a jab of my own. It wasn't hard. It didn't have to be. It connected with his nose and he staggered backward, collapsing into the chair again. I didn't think his nose was broken, but a trickle of blood started leaking out.

"Just tell me the name, Wiggins."

He stared at me in shock. Finally, he said, "I don't know who they are. Not really." He paused, lowered his eyes, and a shudder went through him. "God, what I mess I've made."

"What can you tell me? How did it start?"

"A case I was working. Not even a real case, really. There was a kid that got pinched for possession a couple years ago. We got to talking, and I felt bad for him. No record and he seemed like a good kid, so I cut him loose. A couple weeks later, he finds me at this bar. Wants to thank me for giving him a second chance and says there's somebody he wants me to meet. Next thing I know, this guy is talking to me about how good cops are hard to find and how he has connections to an organization that gives scholarships and shit. I signed Donny up and things seemed good. Then the favors started coming in. Little things at first. Answers to questions, inside information on the department, that sort of thing. It seemed pretty harmless. But things snowballed. The favors got bigger and I realized this 'scholarship' was a loan to be paid back in other ways. The first time I refused, Donny had an accident at school. They made sure I knew it wasn't a co-incidence."

"Who was the guy that set up the scholarship?"

"Said his name was Michael, but that was probably a lie too."

"How do they contact you?"

"Phone. Blocked number."

"Ever try to trace it?"

He shook his head. "Didn't want to risk it."

"Okay," I said. ""Donny's gonna flunk out. You know that, right?"

He looked at me sharply.

"Maybe not this semester, but the next one for sure. You'd know if you saw his Facebook page."

He sighed.

"So my question is: Do you want to make things right?"

He looked away. After a few seconds, he nodded.

"Good. The next time they contact you, I want to know about it. You do what you always do but let me know right away what they want, and I'll pick up the investigation. Off the record."

"Might be a while. Sometimes I don't hear from them for months."

"I'm a patient man."

When I left Wiggins's apartment, I felt good—better than I'd felt in a long time. One case was closed, a fat paycheck was on the way, I saw a future with Stacy, and had a good lead on those responsible for Frank's death. The Christmas spirit settled on me as I drove away, and I found myself singing along with Bing Crosby on the radio.

Nancy was waiting for me when I got to her house. The girls were already in bed, so I placed the gifts under the tree while Nancy brought me a cup of hot chocolate.

"You look different," she said.

"I feel different," I admitted.

We sat on the couch and sipped the cocoa. The tree lights sparkled. It was good to be home.

Epilogue

"He just left," said the silky voice on the phone.

"We must assume our asset is compromised," said Michael. "Proceed."

The line went dead, and Michael put the phone back in his pocket. He wasn't sure about her convictions or how long she would remain loyal, but he was sure she would see this through.

The woman slipped from the car and strode through the night toward the high-rise. She wasn't worried about the cameras in the lobby and there weren't any on the residential floors. The elevator doors slid open. She rode up to the eleventh floor, found the correct apartment, and knocked.

The door opened a crack and Donald Wiggins peered out. She could smell the alcohol on his breath. A trickle of drying blood stained his upper lip.

"You? What are you doing here?"

She'd been here before, of course. He called and she came. But he hadn't called this time. Of course, he was con-fused.

"Consider it my gift for the season," she said.

Comprehension dawned in his eyes and he smiled. He opened the door and let her inside. She took his hand and led him to the recliner and pushed him down into it. He didn't resist.

She straddled him and lowered herself onto his lap. She ground her hips into him. He licked his lips. "This is un-expected," he muttered.

"I'm full of surprises," she said.

Then she opened herself up to him. His energy poured into her. At first, he gave it willingly, letting her drink it up, not knowing what was happening, reveling in the falling sensation. But as the life continued to flow out of him, he instinctively tried to pull back. She wouldn't let him. This was what she did. There was no escaping his fate now.

Wiggins bucked and squirmed as the last of his life force was pulled from him. She soaked it up. All of it. His heart slowed, but before it stopped, she grabbed his head and twisted with all her strength. His neck snapped like a twig. The medical examiner would have no reason to ques-tion the cause of death now.

She stood, straightened her skirt, and disappeared back into the night.

Acknowledgements

I have a few more people to thank for helping make this book a reality. I did a lot of research to make sure I got things right. Lieutenant Jeremy Campbell with the Staunton Police Department was hugely helpful in answering a lot of questions about various police procedures. Also in terrifying me with stories about real life crimes. Prior Peter Funk was gracious enough to give me a virtual tour of the Monastery of the Holy Cross and answer questions about their daily life.

My beta readers deserve thanks as well. Aaron Hale, Erin Bradner, and Symmonie Preston: your feedback was invaluable.

Most of all, I'd like to thank Rachel Brune, who served as my Alpha Reader and developmental editor. She found a number of plot holes and made some excellent suggestions to improve the mess I made. She's also a talented author in her own right. You'd probably enjoy her books as well. Start with Cold Run.

Also, I'd like to thank you. Thanks for going on this little adventure with me. I'm guessing if you're still reading at this point, you enjoyed the story. I'd love to hear from you, whether its through a review, a comment on my Facebook page, or even an email. Without readers like you, this book wouldn't exist.

If you'd like to get a free Mason Gray short story,

head over to my website, www.williamcmarkham.wee-
bly.com to sign up for my mailing list. Thanks again!

About the Author

William lives in the beautiful Shenandoah Valley of Virginia with his wife and four children. He is an elementary school teacher and actor. He performs regularly in a Murder Mystery Dinner Theatre at a local resort and owns a traveling theatre company, Impressions Theatre, that performs in libraries during the summer. He holds a B.S. In Fisheries Science from Virginia Tech and an M.A. In Teaching from Mary Baldwin.

The idea for this novel came to him during a six-year period of time when he lived in Chicago pursuing a professional acting career.

For more information and updates on the next MASON GRAY CASE, visit his website at:
http://williamcmarkham.weebly.com